Kung Fu Gladiator Volume 1

Kung Fu Gladiator
Quest for the Da Qin

By Ben Doublett

COPYRIGHT © 2016 by Ben Doublett
COVER ART © Dennis Menese
COVER & BOOK DESIGN - Moriah Pearson

Published in the United States of America
All Rights Reserved

TABLE OF CONTENTS

CHAPTER ONE •••• PAGE FIVE

CHAPTER TWO •••• PAGE TWENTY-ONE

CHAPTER THREE •••• PAGE THIRTY-FIVE

CHAPTER FOUR •••• PAGE FORTY-NINE

CHAPTER FIVE •••• PAGE SIXTY-THREE

CHAPTER SIX •••• PAGE SEVENTY-SEVEN

AUTHOR'S NOTE •••• PAGE EIGHTY-SEVEN

AUTHOR'S BIO •••• PAGE NINETY-ONE

CHAPTER ONE
103 CE

Li Zhao stumbles from the darkened enclave. Heavy iron chains clank against his ankles, a wall of sunlight blinds him, and a noise like the battle cry of a great army assaults his ears. As his eyes adjust, he realizes it is not an army, but a cheering crowd larger than any assembly of civilians he has ever seen. The crowd is stacked in rows — one behind the other — up and up and up a building the size of a mountain, scattered with red banners and shaded by immense awnings.

The older and larger of the two men Li Zhao is chained to shuffles forward, and Zhao is forced to follow. He brings his gaze down from the stands to his immediate surroundings, the sand under his bare feet is coarse and white. He is standing in some sort of sunken arena, and the attention of the massive crowd is upon him and his current companions. There are half a dozen other trios of men chained together at the ankles — all stripped naked except for a brief loin cloth — clutching awkwardly-shaped iron swords worn with rust, similar to those that Zhao and his companions had been given moments ago. Zhao touches the edge of his blade, it is not sharp. He scrapes it against his thigh, it doesn't even break the skin.

The noise from the spectators rises as more men — glittering in polished armor and oddly shaped helms with colorful plumes — enter the arena. They raise painted shields and brandish weapons that are almost certainly sharper than Zhao's. Their armor is odd, it covers the wrong parts of the body: the sword arm, the shins, the head — but not the torso or the thighs. These vulnerable points are covered only by oil, displaying muscular legs and chests.

The first chained man dies when one of the warriors puts a spear into his abdomen with a quick, practiced thrust. Zhao shudders at the immediacy of it as the cold reality of his situation dawns on him. He realizes he is supposed to die here and now. One of those chained to the dead man lunges forward and swings his sword at the spearman, but the spearman punches the dull blade effortlessly away with a small round shield and kicks the attacker back. He frees his spear from the dead man and whips it around, slashing the attacker across the chest with the sharp point. Blood from both men stains the white sand. Another armored warrior wielding a short sword in each hand kills both remaining members of the trio in a single motion, swinging his sharp blades in an X. This elicits a huge surge in the cheers of the crowd.

Pairs of armored warriors square off with trios of chained men. The chained men are being hacked to pieces everywhere Zhao looks. A spearman and a helmeted warrior brandishing a square shield and broad, double-edged sword storm towards Zhao and his partners. The swordsman points his weapon directly at Zhao and pretends to drag it across his own throat in gesture so dramatic that it must be meant for the crowd. Zhao turns to his companions.

"Friends, stay behind me. I'll try to protect you," he tells them in Greek. Zhao does his best to keep the tremble out of his voice. "Don't attempt to attack. Your blades are dull, you'll only expose yourselves. Stay close, I'll need as much mobility as possible."

"What are you talking about?" The older of the two men spits back, also in Greek. "You can't protect anyone! Don't you understand we're all about to die?"

"Perhaps," Zhao says. "All things happen as they will, it's for us to accept them without resistance. But I don't intend to die here today." His words are spoken to himself as much as they are to the other men. He breathes deeply and focuses on calming his mind, on finding his center.

"Your intent? What's that matter? Look at the size of them!"

"They are indeed large," Zhao agrees. Each of the warriors stands a head or more above him.

They bulge with muscle and fat, as if they both eat and exercise to excess.

Zhao looks at the other man to whom he is chained. He is young and frail, gazing at his thumbs and muttering frantic prayers in a language unfamiliar to Zhao. He shows no sign of even being aware of Zhao's presence.

Before the other man can reply, the warriors are on them. Neither of Zhao's partners had heeded his advice and moved behind him, so the trio presents the warriors with a straight line. The younger man to Zhao's right dies first as the spearman plunges his weapon through his throat so hard that the point emerges behind his head. The swordsman who had gestured at Zhao feints to attack him, but then swings at the older man to Zhao's left. The older man parries the blow with his own sword, but the warriors gleaming steel bites deeply into the prisoner's soft, rusted iron. The warrior then punches the prisoner with the bronze boss of his shield and spins in a circle, swinging his weapon in an elaborate arc as he brings it around to cut the older man's throat. The white sand is sprayed with bright red blood.

It is an ostentatious and impractical way to strike with a sword, Zhao thinks, but the crowd roars their approval. These are showmen, he realizes. They are trained fighters, yes, but they are also playing to the audience. This is mock combat with real death — bloodshed as entertainment. On guard, in true battle, such skilled warriors might pose some difficulty. Especially two at a time, armed with superior weapons. But here and now, they think Zhao is just another lamb to be slaughtered. Good.

The swordsman raises his blade above his head, preparing to deliver another strike for the benefit of the crowd. Zhao darts forward, closing the gap before the blade can begin its arc downward. Fast as a cat, Zhao's left hand wraps the swordsman's wrist in an inescapable grip, and Zhao's right palm lands flat on the underside of his elbow. In a single fluid motion, Zhao rotates the man's arm back, forcing him to flip and land on his knees. Zhao tucks the heavily armored sword arm between his legs. The linen padding and bronze plates do nothing to protect the arm when Zhao twists and breaks it at the shoulder, elbow, and wrist. The gleaming sword drops to the ground and the warrior cries out in pain and shock.

A spear flies at Zhao's face and he bends backwards and to the side, contorting his body and avoiding the thrust at the last moment. The spearman is slow to pull his weapon back and telegraphs exactly where he plans to place it next, so Zhao avoids the second thrust with ease. The warrior aims his third thrust toward Zhao's left side. Faster than thought, Zhao's hand shoots out and makes contact with the shaft of the spear, redirecting the thrust rather than grabbing or blocking. The spearman put all his weight behind the attack and plunges forward. When the warrior's spear makes contact with nothing but air, Zhao takes advantage and spins into him.

"Ki-ya!" Zhao lets out a fearsome shout as he plunges the point of his elbow into the solar plexus of the spearman.

Zhao feels the warrior deflate, like a pierced wineskin, as his elbow sinks into the bundle of nerves. He drops the shield and spear and slumps over. The only thing holding up the slack mass of armor and muscle is the sharp point of Li Zhao's elbow.

Zhao steps aside after a moment and the warrior drops to the sand. Without missing a beat, Zhao picks up the discarded straight sword and hacks the feet from his dead partners, slipping their restraints off. It frees him of their bodies, but not the iron manacle around his own foot or the heavy iron chain that runs through the loop in it.

Zhao looks around the arena floor to see how the other prisoners are faring. A few pairs of warriors are still toying with their bloodied victims, but not one of the chained trios appear to have inflicted so much as a scratch on the warrior pairs. Yet as he searches, a hush falls over the crowd.

Zhao looks up to see a wave of faces turning towards him, the realization that he has defeated his opponents spreading over the mass of people like a ripple across a pond.

The other warriors soon notice what has happened. They see their two compatriots on the ground, one passed out and the other writhing in pain while clutching his ruined arm. Two pairs of armored warriors come towards Zhao at a fast trot: one more spearman, two with helmets and wickedly hooked knives, and one oddly armed man with a net in one hand and a trident in the other. The man with the trident has no helmet, baring locks of shocking red hair and a thick and short red beard.

Zhao turns his attention to the abandoned weapons. The sword is short with a wide blade, and the handle is polished and ornate with inlaid ivory accents. It's heavy for its size and the grip is unfamiliar to Zhao. The spear is much better. The long, ash shaft is also heavy, and less flexible than the bamboo spear shafts he trained with at the monastery, but it would have to do.

Sandwiching the sword blade between his palms, he hurls it forward from above his head at the oncoming warriors, striking the man with the trident and net. The sword pierces his shoulder and knocks him off his feet. The crowd gasps collectively. Zhao's foot licks out and flicks the spear into the air, he grasps the shaft and twirls it in his hands at half speed to grow accustomed to the weight. Then he moves the spear faster, whipping it around his body, above his head, to either side of him, until the spear becomes a blurred circle moving faster than the eye can follow.

The three warriors slow as their companion falls and Zhao performs his spear tricks. Zhao smiles to himself and leaps forward to the knifeman on the far right. The spear shoots out and Zhao feints a blow to the knifeman's helm, sticking the point into the exposed stomach once the shield instinctively goes up. Spinning out of this blow, Zhao strikes the second knifeman across the thighs with the shaft of the spear, knocking him forward but breaking the spear's shaft in the process. Using the remaining shaft of the spear as a vaulting pole, Zhao plunges the weapon into the buttock of the fallen knifeman and launches himself forward in a flying sidekick at the remaining spearman. The iron chain around his ankles slows him, but the kick still lands on the warrior's head and dents his helmet. The spearman wavers for a second, stunned, while Zhao recovers his footing. Zhao leaps forward with a second sidekick, this one landing at the base of his exposed spine with a satisfying crack.

Silence falls across the arena's landscape. Thousands, probably tens of thousands of people and all of them silent. Then a single, ecstatic cheer. A couple more follow and soon the whole stadium is erupting in jubilant cheers. Zhao surveys the scene in front of him, amazed. What kind of people are these, he wonders, to thirst for a man's blood one moment, only to find joy in his shedding of the blood of others in the next? Do they not care that the champions they exhorted only moments ago now lie bloodied and injured?

Zhao reminds himself he is not yet finished with this strange episode. He cannot allow his mind to wander if he is to survive. There are three remaining pairs of warriors and they are all converging on him, encircling him, and he is unarmed once again.

One of the remaining warriors, who wields a sword in each hand and is wearing no helmet, shouts something in Latin. Zhao knows little of that language and cannot understand the words, but the tone sounds like a command. The encirclement separates Zhao from all but the spear of the warrior he had just defeated, and even reaching for that would expose him to attack. A second command comes from the dual-sword wielder, and the other five warriors lurch forward at once.

Zhao's manacled foot flicks up high and the chain lands in his right hand. The heavy, round manacles from the other prisoners are affixed to either end, but the chain can slide easily through the wide loop in Zhao's manacle. Zhao hurls it forward and one manacle strikes an approaching net-and-trident warrior in his unarmored face. The warrior falls back and Zhao swings the chain in a wide arc, whipping it across the others at head-level. He strikes them all, knocking out the two others with unprotected heads and delivering ringing blows to the two who wore helmets. Zhao recalls the makeshift chain whip and spins it across his neck and by his side, gaining momentum, and then kicks it forward. The manacle smashes into the raised shield of a helmeted swordsman, tearing through painted rawhide and splintering wood, cracking the warrior's bare collarbone.

The second helmeted warrior lunges forward with his short, hooked knife, but Zhao jumps out of the path of his cut. He skips back two long steps, whipping the chain around as he does and wrapping it around the knifeman's armored shin. Zhao jerks hard on the chain, pulling the warrior's leg out from under him. The warrior falls flat on his back as Zhao leaps to an impossible height. He comes crashing down, putting all of his weight into the point of his knee, driving it hard into the bare, muscled chest. Zhao feels bone and muscle give as the warrior lets out a pitiful grunt.

Now only the dual sword-wielder remains.

He raises his swords to his sides, directing his attention to the crowd that is once again silent and holding their collective breath. He moves the swords up and down, and they start to cheer and howl. The warrior next places one blade behind his ear and leans to the side, as if to indicate that he cannot hear them. His histrionic gesturing receives an almost immediate reaction from the crowd. Their roars become a chant that is ambiguous at first, but they slowly form a discernable name.

"His-pan-i-cus! His-pan-i-cus! His-pan-i-cus!"

Hispanicus, as if rewarding them for their cheers, begins to twirl his swords impressively. He strikes the blades against one another, creating little sparks, showing off his dexterity and eliciting sounds of awe from his audience.

Hispanicus bellows something in a tongue Zhao does not recognize. When Zhao does not respond, Hispanicus roars with laughter, and Zhao can see he is as impressed with himself as the crowd is.

"Sun Tzu said, 'Remove the firewood from under the pot,'" Zhao whispers, in his own language.

Zhao raises his chain and begins to swing it. His training at the monastery had included the art of the jiujiebian, and he begins to execute the most complex form he knows with that weapon. The chain twirls about him as he darts across the sand, swinging it under his feet, to his sides, around his neck, his thighs, his arms, speeding it up until the chain itself transforms into a greyish shroud surrounding his body. It is everywhere and nowhere at once.

The chants of 'Hispanicus' begin to fade as Zhao proceeds, stealing their approval from the warrior, taking the firewood from under his pot. As his form nears its end, Zhao breaks from it and sends his chain rocketing forward.

Hispanicus raises one of his blades to block, which is exactly what Zhao anticipated him to do. The chain wraps around the blade, and Zhao jerks back, pulling the sword out of Hispanicus' grip. The crowd erupts again, but this time into laughter – mocking laughter.

Zhao pantomimes, offering the sword back to Hispanicus, and the crowd jeers at the warrior they were cheering moments ago. Hispanicus' bare face reddens.

"You seem temperamental!" Zhao shouts over the din of the crowd. "Sun Tzu said, 'If your opponent is temperamental, seek to irritate him.'"

Hispanicus roars something in response that Zhao does not understand.

Zhao tosses the sword back, allowing it to land in the space between them, offering Hispanicus a bait. Hispanicus takes it, rushing forward for the sword, and Zhao responds by shooting the chain whip out. It strikes hard at the ground between the warrior and the sword, forcing him to scamper back to more acclamations from the audience. The warriors in this display clearly value the opinion of the crowd, and Zhao was winning them over with every move.

Zhao chases Hispanicus, swinging his chain whip in a wide figure-eight, spinning to gain momentum, refusing to ever let the warrior gain his footing. Then Zhao telegraphs a long, arcing strike to Hispanicus' vulnerable head, leaving the warrior no choice but to block with his remaining sword, even if he understands Zhao's ploy.

The chain whip entangles Hispanicus last weapon, but this time he refuses to let go. He grasps the handle with both hands and tugs Zhao towards him.

The crowd erupts into new bouts of laughter at the spectacle of the giant gladiator engaging in a tug of war for his own sword with the much smaller prisoner. Zhao, knowing he is no match for Hispanicus in a contest of pure strength, releases the chain from his hands and half jumps, half runs at Hispanicus, allowing the warrior to stumble back under his own momentum. As Zhao rushes Hispanicus, he scoops up the sword that had been dropped between them, and uses it to strike Hispanicus' own blade from his hand, then presses the tip of the sword to his throat. Hispanicus is now at his mercy.

The warrior stares up at Zhao, fire burning in his eyes. Then Zhao retracts the sword and, with an open palm, slaps Hispanicus across the face – causing more laughter to spill from the crowd. Zhao skitters back, laughing himself, as Hispanicus lunges forward. He appears to intend to throttle Zhao with his bare hands but a trumpet sounds and Hispanicus stops in his tracks, turning to the raised platform at the front of the stadium and standing rigidly at attention. The cheers and cries of the crowd suddenly die down to a low murmur. A man stands in the platform's box, draped in purple silken robes, one hand across his chest, the other raised out with the palm facing the crowd. It is hard to tell from this distance, but to Zhao the man appears to be smiling.

He speaks some words in Latin that Zhao cannot understand, and the words are repeated by men stationed all across the stadium. They are the loudest voices Zhao has ever heard. The crowd roars again, sounding pleased. The swordsman bows his head and retreats across the arena, but not before casting a glare at Zhao, the meaning of which transcends any language barrier. "Next time," it says, "I will kill you."

"That was the best pregame show since the Secular Games! Where did you learn to fight like that? I bet it was Capua. All that jumping and prancing about, it looked like you were dancing! It was the most supreme display of skill I've ever seen!"

"It was not," Li Zhao replies.

The earnest young Roman blurting out a torrent of words at Zhao in Greek wears, over his short sleeved tunic, the heavy plain white linen garment known as the toga. It is wrapped in several delicate folds around his waist and draped expertly across one shoulder. Zhao knows that in these lands only adult men are permitted to wear the toga, but this boy standing before Zhao is hardly old enough to have shaved his first beard and has the excitable demeanor of an adolescent. Standing at the edge of the room is an old man dressed in a clean but simple tunic, wearing a collar that denotes his status as a slave. Zhao had been lead to the room in which they now stand after he was dismissed from the arena and ordered to wait there. His manacle has been chained to the wall as insurance for if he tried to disobey that order. It is the same room where Zhao had been chained to the other prisoners before they were shoved down a hall and out onto the killing field. The air in the room is thick and humid, smelling of stale sweat.

"What do you mean it was not? I've been watching the games since before I could walk and you just pulled off the biggest upset I've ever seen. You're going to make me richer than Crassus."

"Sun Tzu said, 'The supreme art of war, the acme of excellence, is to defeat the enemy without fighting.' I was compelled to fight in order to defeat my enemy today. This is not a supreme display of skill," Zhao says. Then he adds, "Pardon, but how am I to make you rich?"

"How do you think? I'm your new owner. Tiberius is the name, Tiberius Lentilus. I'm a lanista."

"My . . . owner?"

"Yes! Didn't you hear old Trajan up there?" Tiberius says, just as another man walks into the room.

Zhao tenses — it is another warrior. He wears a bronze helm with a bright blue plume and a broad brim, like a hat, a visor is pulled down over his face. Zhao's eyes scan the room for anything that can be used as a weapon but sees nothing.

The warrior, however, does not even glance at Zhao. He says something quietly to the little Tiberius Lentilus in Latin and Tiberius snaps his fingers, prompting the old slave behind him to hand him a clay tablet, which Tiberius examines for a moment. Tiberius points back down the hall and says a few Latin words in reply, then the warrior turns and departs.

"Emperor Trajan himself pardons you and you don't even pay attention," Tiberius mutters, switching back to Greek.

"The purple-clad man, I inferred he was of some importance. He is the Emperor of the Da Qin?" Zhao asks, his voice picking up a note of urgency. Tiberius nods. "And yet he appears before the public, as if he were any normal minister or state official. Fascinating. Quickly, take me to him. I have an important matter I must bring to his attention."

Tiberius laughs. Zhao's face remains impassive.

"Oh you're . . . you're serious? No, I'm not going to take you to the Emperor," he says. "It's not Saturnalia, I'm not taking orders from my own slaves."

"You are mistaken, friend. I am no slave."

"Yes, you are," the Roman youth insists, exasperation creeping into his voice. "I heard the Emperor pronounce it myself."

"I . . . I did not understand him. He spoke Latin and, of Western tongues, I have only Greek."

"Greek is an Eastern tongue," Tiberius replies, with the tone of strained patience one might employ when speaking to an idiot.

"The Greek-speaking world is to the west of my homeland."

Another warrior enters the room, this one carrying a spear. "No, no, no, the hoplomachi are assembling on the other side of the arena," Tiberius says to the man in Greek as soon as he walks in. "Turn around and go back the way you came."

"Yes, Master. Sorry, Master," the warrior replies, and leaves with a little bow.

Zhao is struck by the use of the warrior's word 'master.' These warriors, skilled and massive as they are, could they really all be slaves?

"Where exactly is that homeland? You have a strange look to you," Tiberius asks, turning back to Zhao and carefully studying his face. "I've seen foreign slaves come and go through the ludus all my life, but I've never seen one with eyes and hair like yours. The closest would be Scythian, I guess. Is that it? Or some Parthian Satrapy far to the east? Or is it India? I've never met an Indian but I heard they're brown skinned."

"I am of Zhongguo. The Middle Kingdom. China."

"Never heard of it," Tiberius says, taking a tablet and a heavy bronze stylus from his slave and making some kind of mark on it.
"You may know it as Serica."

Tiberius drops the stylus and spins at Zhao. "You're from Serica? I didn't think that place even existed!"

"It does," Zhao says.

"Wow. But I suppose that explains why you look so alien. Serica. That's even further than Alexander went, right? Further east than India or Bactria?"

Zhao nods.

"Wow, Serica. That's incredible. You know, I spoke to an Arabian merchant one time and he insisted that Serica's a real place. I didn't believe him, of course. Arabians are all liars, you know."

The Roman youth pauses, as if waiting for Zhao to agree, but when he gets no response he continues.

"Well, this Arabian said he sails to India sometimes and that he talked to an Indian who had done business with some island trader who made one trip to Serica and came back with enough silk to set himself up for life. And you made the whole trip from Serica to Rome yourself! From one end of the world to the other. Incredible. Are you some kind of merchant?"

"No," Zhao says.

"Shame. A bolt of silk must pass through a hundred different hands before it reaches Rome, each trader putting his own little markup on it. Imagine if you could collect all that profit yourself. You'd be rich enough to buy all the gold in Iberia. Say, is it true that silk is just growing on trees out there? And people go around plucking it like leaves?"

"No, this is not true," Zhao says.

"I didn't think so. Does it come from giant spiders? That same Arabian told me it came from spiders as big as dogs."

Zhao tells him no again.

"I knew that bastard was a liar. Never trust an Arabian. So you must have been a gladiator back in Serica, huh?"

"I was . . ." Zhao considers his response for a moment. "I was a soldier when I left."

"A soldier? Can all Serican soldiers fight like you?"

"I am one of the more rigorously trained soldiers of the Han Emperor."

"Well, you're not a soldier anymore. You're a gladiator now. Trajan said it would be a crime to deny the people another show like the one you just put on. First time I've ever seen someone in the execution shows get a

17

pardon. Don't get too cocky though, they were all amateurs except Hispanicus. The one you killed was mine, so I got your title as compensation."

Zhao does not reply or respond to Tiberius. He takes a couple steps back and slumps on the rough wooden bench, the only furnishing in the cramped, smelly room.

"Don't worry, I'm a congenial master and the gladiator's life is about as good as it gets for a slave. Some freemen even volunteer for it. You get big meals, beautiful women who pay to sleep with you, fame, adulation, even manumission is possible eventually." Tiberius beams at Zhao. "Some gladiators retire quite rich, too."

"I did not intend to kill any of those men. My aim was only to wound or disable in defense of my own life."

"Oh, is that what's bothering you? Relax. Granicus, the one you killed, was a retiarius, and not a particularly good one at that. You threw the sword at him, remember? They go in bare-headed and unarmored, so they die all the time."

Another warrior enters the room, this one unarmed and naked as the day he was born, but so thick with muscle and fat as to be unmistakably one of the so-called gladiators. Tiberius says something to him in Latin. He lifts his arms and spins, a vacant look in his eyes. Tiberius says something else and the gladiator leaves. "Buy that one," Tiberius says in Greek once he's gone. "Any price that Marcus asks, make sure we get him. He's a three year veteran and didn't have a scratch on him. Fucking goldmine right there."

"Yes, Master," the slave replies.

"Anyway, my contract stipulated that if any of mine were killed by any 'hazards of the arena' I'd be compensated," Tiberius continues. "Of course, by a hazard, they mean a falling rock or loose cheetah, but I told the arena manager a good enough lawyer could easily persuade a jury that prisoners count as hazards. He agreed when I said I'd be willing to take you

18

in lieu of cash. So it actually worked out well for everyone."

Zhao looks at Tiberius pointedly.

"Well, everyone except Granicus, that is."

"I see. I understood that I was condemned to die. I am confused by this, though. Is it your custom to use the execution of all condemned men for such . . . entertainments?"

"Yes. Well, not all men, just foreigners, slaves, provincials, that sort. We don't execute citizens dishonorably. It's pleasing to the dead to have condemned men spill blood in their honor, so we have these fights and dedicate them to notable dead Romans. Or at least that is why we used to do it. Now it's more about pleasing the mob than the dead. Romans are prone to rioting if they aren't fed and entertained."

"This custom . . . it is strange to me. It seems cruel and imbruting."

This comment seems to make Tiberius prickly. "Well, it's not. It's good for the character, helps maintain the old Roman martial spirit and stops us from becoming effeminate like the Greeks or the Persians. Besides, you don't have to like it. You're a slave. If the gods didn't approve of Roman customs, they wouldn't have allowed Rome to conquer half the world, would they?"

Zhao nods. "This is true. If your ways were unjust, your ruler would lose the Mandate of Heaven and fall. The fact that your empire is so great proves that your people are righteous, even if your customs seem strange to me. I am a guest in your land and it's not my place to judge your ways. I apologize."

"Accepted," Tiberius says. "So tell me, how is it that a Serican soldier finds himself condemned to die in a Roman arena, wanting to speak to Emperor Trajan?"

CHAPTER TWO
FIVE YEARS EARLIER
97 CE

The military garrison just outside of the oasis city of Qiuci was heavily fortified with a palisade wall and a series of earthworks and trenches leading up to it, but the natives who lived nearby appeared not to find the presence of the foreign military force intrusive. Rather, true to their mercantile reputation, the locals had been doing a brisk trade serving the Chinese soldiers. The area surrounding the fortifications was filled with the smells of cooking and the shouts of merchants crying their wares.

Ban Chao, the Protector General of the Western Regions, cut an impressive figure. Tall and robust with a barrel chest and quick, intelligent eyes. If it were not for the gray in his long beard and hair, Captain Li Zhao would never have known General Ban Chao was well into his sixties. The last time Zhao had seen Ban Chao, he had been in heavy armor, but now he wore long, red and black silk robes inlaid with gold thread and a wide black sash was tied across his ample midsection.

"General Gan Ying, you old dog!" Ban Chao declared, clapping his hands on the shoulders of Li Zhao's master as General Gan Ying attempted a formal bow with his left fist enclosed in his right palm. "How have you been the past few months? I hear half the whores in Chang'an have been going hungry since you left!"

"I have been very well, Protector General," Gan Ying said as Ban Chao's embrace caught him mid-bow.

Captain Li Zhao stifled a smile at his master's discomfiture. Zhao stood at perfect attention, leading the company of soldiers who served as General Gan Ying's personal guard.

"Oh, forgive me," Ban Chao said, with a vast, jovial smile. "I'm afraid I've become a bit of a boor living out here on the Western frontier. Pretty soon I'll be as barbarous as the natives, fucking goats and drinking rotten milk. Anyway, come on in, old friend, judging from your letter we've got a lot to discuss."

Ban Chao led Gan Ying into a nearby tent where the two generals could confer privately. Zhao marched his company behind Gan Ying and indicated that they were to take up position around the tent with a series of hand signals. His men followed the silent orders as if they had been shouted.

A young soldier pushing a wheelbarrow full of repeating crossbow stocks almost ran into Zhao, but the captain stepped aside at the last moment. The young man cast Zhao a brief, apologetic glance and hurried on his way. Other men pushed past, some fully armed heavy infantry men, others in light robes carrying bundles of swords or crossbow bolts or pulling carts of freshly laundered clothes.

Zhao positioned himself close to the tent that Gan Ying had just entered, hoping to hear as much as he could. He removed his helmet and placed it on the ground next to his feet so that his hearing was unobstructed. Zhao, like the men of his company, wore iron scale armor over a thickly padded linen battle dress that came down to his mid-shins. His men were armed with tightly woven wicker shields and skirmishing spears, but Zhao himself carried only a long, straight sword at his side. The hammering of a nearby smith rang in Zhao's ears, but the fabric walls of the tent were not thick and Zhao could hear what was being said inside.

"It's been very quiet out here since I gave the Yanqi that second defeat. I'd say the region has been completely pacified," Zhao heard Ban Chao say. "The Kushans haven't made a peep since I forced them to give up that shit show of an invasion seven years ago. More than fifty kings, petty and great, have come to me to pledge fealty. I'm running out of families to place all the hostages with! We've done more than enough already, Gan Ying, and I'm getting old. I see no need for this new adventure."

"But, Protector General, don't you want to know more about the West?"

"I know what's to the west!" Ban Chao's thunderous voice declared. "Barbarians, barbarians, and more barbarians. Legends aside, all you'll find in that direction will be barbarians. And the farther west you travel, the more barbarous they'll become."

"That's what people thought before Zhang Qian's journeys," Gan Ying said, in a much quieter, calmer tone. Zhao had to strain to hear his master, but Ban Chao could probably be heard beyond the walls of the encampment. "But look at all Zhang Qian told of in his reports, the places he didn't even visit like Shendu and Da Xia. We're hearing regularly now from merchants and emissaries about an even greater empire to the west, the Da Qin."

"I was as inspired by Zhang Qian's writings as anyone, General. That's why I came out here in the first place! I wanted to be the one who got the kingdoms he discovered to submit to the authority of the Son of Heaven. But I don't put any faith in hearsay from barbarian wanderers or foreign merchants, and neither should you. Besides sailor's stories, do you have any hard proof that the Da Qin Empire even exists?"

Captain Li Zhao smiled to himself when he heard Ban Chao ask this question. He knew exactly what proof Gan Ying had. Zhao heard a jingling sound as Gan Ying emptied the small pack he concealed beneath his robes in front of Ban Chao. After a moment, the senior general spoke.

"What are these?"

23

"Coins," Gan Ying responded. "Some look very old, others are more recent, but they're all struck with the images of the Da Qin emperors. Or at least I think they must be the Da Qin emperors. There are many different faces, so either their emperor changes frequently or he allows the lords and kings below him to mint coins in their own images."

"Interesting. They look more like Kushan coins than ours, with one of their gods on one side and the king or emperor on the other, but no hole for stringing coins together. And these were hammered, not cast. "

"Yes, but the artistry is superior to the Kushan coins, don't you think? I suspect the Kushan coins are imitations they made after seeing the Da Qin ones. And look at the writing — it's an entirely different kind of script than what's used by the Kushans. Or any other people I know of, for that matter."

"This gold one has a woman on it!" Ban Chao cried. "Look, she's on the same side of the coin as their emperor, facing him. Like an equal! What kind of people disrespect their rulers like that?"

"That's exactly what I'm going to find out, Protector General," Gan Ying said, the excitement in his voice rising. "For years and years, I've been collecting these coins from foreign merchants who've been to ports all over the world. I've also been collecting tales. Everyone seems to agree that the territory of the Da Qin is at the western end of the world, and that their empire is vast and diverse. But there are so many things we don't know about them. How do they choose their kings? How does one read their writing? How much will they pay for silk? What knowledge do they have that we don't? What knowledge do we have that we might teach them? My mission will answer these questions. But we can be certain of their existence already."

Ban Chao was silent for a long time. Li Zhao had begun to worry that Gan Ying's plea may have fallen flat when Ban Chao spoke again, slowly and thoughtfully.

"I come from a family of distinguished scholars and historians. They've all served the emperor well in their capacity, but when my father and brother pressured me to take up the writing brush instead of the sword, I refused. I told them both, 'A brave man has no other plan but to walk in the footsteps of Zhang Qian, to do great deeds and build a great reputation in a distant, foreign land. How can I waste my life on writing?' It was Zhang Qian's quest that inspired me to devote my life to extending the authority of the Son of Heaven as far west as the setting sun."

"But now, in my old age," Ban Chao continued, "I've become too comfortable, too cynical. I've seen too much blood spilled, on the battlefield and off. Taming this savage region has made me see that, in the same way clear water cannot succor a great fish, clean governance cannot foster the harmony of governed peoples. I've had to cause much suffering as Protector General of the Western Regions. I've had to order the deaths of innocents, destroy homes, starve women and children. You're younger than me, Gan Ying, and, I hope you won't mind my saying, a little naïve. But you've got the same yearning for adventure I had before I came out here."

Ban Chao paused and Zhao leaned in closer.

"I've made my decision," Ban Chao said. "I won't stop you from pursuing this dream, Gan Ying. Take your company of soldiers as bodyguards. I'll arrange for some educated men to go with you as well. Just make sure you come back alive and with some good stories, and, if you can, the good will of the Emperor of Da Qin."

Gan Ying and his party rode out a week later, having stocked up on enough provisions to supply the company of soldiers, as well as Gan Ying's small party of scholars and assistants, for several months. Only Gan Ying and Captain Li Zhao knew how much gold and silver was in the concealed, locked chest on the back of one of their heavy-laden Bactrian camels. Zhao could not conceive of how anyone could aim to spend such an amount in a lifetime, let alone on a single mission.

For himself, Zhao had packed three swords, a bow and arrows, additional rations of rice and tea, and a bolt of silk he planned to sell in the westernmost region they visited. He had heard from many of the merchants he had interviewed with his master that the people of the Da

Qin would pay exorbitant prices for the fabric and so, while Zhao was no professional trader, he thought this modest investment might be worth making. He had also packed large quantities of paper and ink to record his observations as they traveled.

Zhao had wanted to bring more personal supplies but his horse was not up to carrying the burden. The poor brown stallion was a little thin and his coat was as patchy as a dog with mange. Zhao resolved to walk on foot for most of the journey, using the beast more like a pack mule than a mount. He had never been comfortable sitting on a horse. The scholars in the party all rode on horseback for now, as did Gan Ying. Several large, two-humped Bactrian camels with long, almost feminine eyelashes carried most of their baggage. Five other soldiers were mounted, as were the five hired Kushan guides, but the rest of the company were light infantry with five crossbow teams.

The five cavalrymen marched at the head of the party and the light infantry brought up the rear, with the scholars and Gan Ying. The Kushan guides took turns riding ahead in pairs, swinging back infrequently to report on the safety of the route and trade duties with their counterparts. Zhao himself walked his horse alongside Gan Ying.

"Finally, we're finally doing it, Captain. After all these years, I cannot believe we are finally going to contact the Da Qin!" Gan Ying said.

"It has been a long time coming, sir. I know how important this mission is to you. I can only hope that I prove worthy to serve you as you conduct it," Zhao said.

"Nonsense! This is as much your mission as it is mine, Captain. You're the one who spent years in every port town along the coast asking for foreign merchants, sifting through foreign coins, annotating my interviews with mercenaries and emissaries, and poring over the reports of Zhang Qian to find some overlooked sentence or phrase that might give us more information about the Da Qin. I could no more take this journey without you than you could without me."

Zhao smiled up at his master. He had never seen Gan Ying in such high spirits.

"Do you realize that men will write of what we have set out to do today a thousand years from now? The peoples of the Earth have been scattered, Li Zhao. Everyone knows about the ancient Sage Kings, but I have a theory of my own. I think the Sage Kings didn't only rule the Middle Kingdom. I think they ruled the entire world, as far west as the westernmost shores of the Da Qin Empire."

Li Zhao nodded his agreement. He had heard this all before, but Gan Ying was speaking more to himself than to Zhao.

"Once the Da Qin and the Han are reunited, the whole world can be brought under the same rule again. Everyone will follow the same just laws. Trade will flourish and enrich the common people materially. Knowledge will spread and enrich the gentlemen spiritually. The barbarian menace will be stomped out. The first Qin and Han Emperors ended the Warring States period and brought peace to millions, but even that pales in comparison to what could be achieved as a result of our mission. Imagine, an end to all war, universal peace under a universal emperor."

"I hope you will not tell the emperor of the Da Qin that it is your purpose to subordinate him to the Son of Heaven," Li Zhao said.

Gan Ying laughed. "Don't be silly, Captain! We are just going to establish relations with the Da Qin. The reunification of the world will come much, much later. Decades from now, maybe centuries. Our entire quest is but the first step on a journey of ten thousand li."

"Confucius said, 'It does not matter how slowly you go, as long as you do not stop,'" Li Zhao said.

The days blended together as the caravan slowly skirted the vast, dry grasslands at the northern edge of the Tarim Basin. Li Zhao spent most of the journey next to Gan Ying, whose conversation was as monotonous as the terrain. Gan Ying had still not gotten over his initial excitement about their mission and continued to talk about its importance with the enthusiasm of a young child. Many men may have found the general tiresome, but Li Zhao had served Gan Ying long enough to understand the full importance of their undertaking to him. Gan Ying was a man of great vision and passion who saw the world as a place of wonder; it was almost impossible for Li Zhao to feel anything towards him but admiration in the best of times and mild amusement at the worst.

"We've been in the grasslands far too long," one of the mounted scholars, a man named Ban Xie, said to Li Zhao as they trudged along. "These Kushans are barbarians, how do we know they haven't gotten us lost?"

"The Kushans are among the greatest trading people in the world, sir," Li Zhao said. "Our guides know this route as well as you know the works of Mencius."

Ban Xie sniffed. He was a distant relative of Ban Chao, and appeared to be fully aware of the prestige of his family name. "Do you have any idea where we are right now?" Ban Xie asked Zhao, without looking down.

"We are taking a northern route around the Taklimakan Desert," Zhao said. "The subject city of Qiuci was the largest city between here and Kashgar, but there will be other smaller cities and settlements along the way. Kashgar is the westernmost kingdom that has paid tribute to Protector General Ban Chao. Once we pass through Kashgar, we will be in a truly foreign land beyond the power of the Son of Heaven — the Kushan Empire."

"I don't trust those Kushan ruffians," Ban Xie said. "I've been reading about them. Zhang Qian asked the Kushans for aid against the Xiongnu and they refused him. They're no friends to the Han people."

"That was two hundred years ago, sir. The Kushans did give Protector General Ban Chao aid in repelling the Kangju from Kashgar only thirteen years ago. The Kushan horse archers proved to be steadfast allies in that conflict."

"Steadfast allies! They marched an army of 70,000 horse archers into Chinese territory after the Kangju were defeated. What kind of an ally does that?" The scholar raised his voice, as if Li Zhao had personally insulted him by daring to have a differing opinion.

"One who has been slighted, sir," Li Zhao replied, keeping his voice as calm as possible. "The Kushan custom is to exchange brides to seal an alliance. When the Kangju were defeated, the Kushans requested a Han princess and the Emperor refused. To the Kushans this was a scurrilous affront, akin to breaking the alliance. Sending an army was, according to their custom, a reasonable response."

"A reasonable response, he says! You think it was reasonable to make war because the Son of Heaven refused to prostitute his daughter to a horse-eating savage?" Ban Xie said.

"Pardon, I was not clear," Li Zhao bowed his head. "I did not offer my own opinion, merely an explanation of what one steeped in Kushan culture would believe to be reasonable. I meant no offense."

The scholar sniffed and raised his nose. "As if I could be offended by the opinion of a mere spear carrier. What's it to me if you don't understand these matters? But you should know better than to attempt to correct educated gentlemen, soldier."

Ban Xie spoke the last word as if it were a slur. Li Zhao bowed his head again but said nothing.

"I can see why these lands are populated by only traders and herders," Gan Ying said to Li Zhao, changing the subject to diffuse the tension. "This soil is terrible. Could you imagine trying to grow millet here?"

"I've not seen any soil fit to grow anything more than grass," Li Zhao agreed. "The ground is parched and barren, yet the people who live here have discovered a way to turn their poor land into the finest horseflesh in the world. It's hard to believe that what we see as a wasteland has —"

A gurgled cry from behind interrupted their conversation, causing both Gan Ying and Li Zhao to whip their heads around.

Two more cries came from the light infantry company in the rear and Zhao saw that they were the cries of men with arrows sunk deep into their bodies, the arrows had pierced straight through their light armor. They were long arrows fletched with eagle feathers that could only have been fired by the heavy, composite bows of the Xiongnu.

The rapidity of the arrow fire picked up and missiles were whizzing towards the party every few seconds. Some of them buzzed right by Zhao's head. One pierced the shoulder of one of the scholars, and the sheer force of the bolt knocked him from his horse. The arrows that missed their targets buzzed by like hornets, those that struck the ground sent shudders through the earth that they felt in their feet.

Zhao's dao, a broadsword with a curved blade and hilt designed for cavalry fighting, was in his hand instantly. With a few quick swipes, he had cut the heavy supply packs off his horse, allowing them to drop to the ground, leaving only a saddle, his bow, and a quiver of arrows. He struggled to mount the horse, his battle dress pulling tightly against his legs as he tried to split them over the horse's back, and digging into him once he had. He tugged on the horse's reigns and maneuvered himself between Gan Ying and the source of the arrows, which were flying from both their rear and their right. An arrow arced towards Gan Ying, but Zhao batted it away with the flat of his sword.

"Infantry, tight formation. Spears at the ready, immediately!" Zhao's voice called out and the soldiers who had been scrambling to raise their wicker shields a second before coalesced, as if the sound of Zhao's voice had activated some instinct buried deep below any individual consciousness.

"Crossbowmen, get behind the infantry and prepare to fire. Infantry, protect the crossbowmen. Cavalry, evacuate the supplies and civilians, now!"

"But, Captain, shouldn't we stay with you? We don't know what's further ahead," one of the cavalrymen objected.

"If there were more ahead, they would have attacked us from that direction, too, and pinned us down. Now move! They'll be on us in a second and if they get an idea of the value of what we're carrying, we'll be fighting off raiders every ten li between here and Kashgar. Go!"

The attackers were the nomads of the grasslands, members of some tributary tribe to the Xiongnu no doubt. They were armored lightly and dissimilarly, but all of them were mounted and expert archers. Sometimes soldiers and sometimes raiders, they preyed upon the merchants who took this route. As the nomad warriors drew closer, their arrows began to pierce the tightly-woven, wicker skirmishing shields of the light infantry phalanx as if they were made of grass. Their bows were powerful, but not as powerful as the five crossbows the company held in reserve. At Li Zhao's signal, the crossbowmen began to fire, unleashing a torrent of solid cast iron bolts at the nomads as they approached, knocking the mounted warriors off their horses.

One particularly well-aimed bolt burst through the knee of a horse, severing the leg completely. Horse and rider tumbled forward in a crash, and the lightly armored rider's body was crushed and contorted under the screaming beast.

At this first show of organized resistance, the nomads turned their horses and scattered in a hasty retreat. Some even wailed and screamed in apparent hysteria. They were close enough when they turned that a few of the infantrymen broke ranks and were able to reach them with their spears. When one spearman gouged the buttocks of an enemy horse, the other infantrymen gave chase, hot with anger at the loss of their companions and eager to get some blood on their weapons in return.

"No, get back in formation! Stop, now!" Zhao cried, to no avail. The blood of the men was up and they had their prey on the run — or so they thought.

They chased the nomads across the plains, hurling sling stones and occasionally hefting their spears as javelins, until half of them were unarmed and scattered.

"Get back in formation!" Zhao cried again, uselessly.

He had seen this stratagem too many times in battle against the Xiongnu to think anything could be done now. Still, he had to try. Zhao urged his horse forward, and galloped at the rapidly closing ranks of the raiders. Before Zhao had closed half the distance, the randomly scattered raiders regrouped like a briefly disturbed flock of birds and ran down the defenseless infantry troops. Some of them were trampled under hooves, others were picked off by arrows. Zhao swatted away the arrows that were fired at him with his broadsword, galloping in and lopping the arm off a raider as he did.

Zhao shouted out a fierce battle cry and urged his horse past their formation, hacking at any nomad within reach, hoping to distract the attackers long enough to give his men the time they would need to reform their ranks. He turned to look behind him — a contingent of the nomads had peeled off, but the rest returned to take out the crossbowmen and the handful of spearman who had not charged in response to the feigned flight with the others. Zhao's horse was galloping as hard as it could but the poor creature was smaller and weaker than the horses of the nomads. They were gaining ground and firing a rapid succession of arrows at him.

An arrow struck Zhao in the back of the shoulder, penetrating the cast iron scales of his armor as if it were paper. The force of the missile knocked him forward and a hot pain seared across his back. He jerked his head up and forced himself on. A deep breath helped him channel his body's vital energy. Zhao envisioned his qi flowing to his arms and legs from its central locus at the pit of his stomach as he had been taught many years ago. Just as the pain was starting to abate, a second arrow buzzed at him, this one shearing skin from the side of his neck but missing its intended mark. He permitted himself a glance over his shoulder and saw that the riders were much closer than he had expected. There were six of them, and all six were riding at a gallop.

Zhao's horse stumbled, its knees hitting the ground hard. Zhao lurched forward, almost coming off. Barely, the horse regained its footing and continued forward slowly, clearly over-burdened by Zhao's weight and the hard burst of speed. The six nomads slowed as well, but not as quickly as Zhao. All of a sudden, he was behind them. Turning the mishap to his advantage, Zhao's own bow was in his hand an instant later. He let fly four arrows in quick succession.

The motion of the horse jostled his aim. Two arrows whizzed far above the head of one nomad, one went wide to the right of its target but the other struck a horse in the rump. Just as he was reaching for another handful of arrows, two of the nomads turned in their saddles without turning their horses, twisting at an impossible angle, and fired at Zhao.

An arrow struck Li Zhao in the chest, another in the shoulder, and then a third. The forth was from a rider that had pulled his mare around in a wide arc and galloped back towards Zhao, firing head-on so that the speed of his horse was added to rather than retracted from that of his arrow. That arrow buzzed through the air fast and straight and struck Zhao in the ribs, knocking him from his horse with the force of a donkey's kick. Then, with the weight of a thousand bars of cast iron, a horse's hoof crashed down on his right leg, just above the knee. Zhao heard a sickening crack and the world blackened.

As he lay splayed out on the dry, patchy grass, waiting for death to come, the last thing Captain Li Zhao saw was Gan Ying and the scholars. By now they were only the size of mice off in the distance, retreating on horseback with a sizeable contingent of nomads catching up to them.

CHAPTER THREE

Li Zhao felt a jerking sensation. Someone was pulling on him. He struggled to open his eyes but could not. Something moved his leg and a deep, skeletal pain rocked his body. He felt himself spasm and let loose a gurgled cry, then the darkness took him again.

He was shaking — rattling. The arrows felt like they were moving around inside him, stretching out his wounds from within, tearing at his flesh. His body was bent over something at the midsection. His eyes cracked open to see the ground beneath him moving. With his nose full of the smell of horse, Zhao realized he was being taken somewhere. He tried to move his legs but they were stuck together — bound — so were his hands. He was slung across the horse's back like a sack of trade goods.

Words could not come to his lips. He willed himself to speak for what seemed like an hour before his parched throat managed to push out a noise.

"St . . . stop. Please stop." Zhao croaked.

A riding crop whistled through the air and struck him on the back in answer.

The ride was unceasing. They kept to a brisk trot, occasionally slowing to a walk, but never stopping. Every step the horse took was a fresh agony to Zhao, sending a new shockwave of pain through his broken leg and ribs. Blood had pooled in his head, making him dizzy to the point of delirium. He vomited frequently, but every time he asked his captors to slow or stop the only answer he would receive was the crack of a riding crop across his back.

The horse Zhao was draped across had no other rider but it kept pace obediently with a group of other horses. Some of the horses were ridden and others were laden with supplies or just trotted along bareback. Zhao could not quite get a good look at any of the riders from his position, he only caught occasional whiffs of putrid smells, both from the horses and the riders. Infrequently, he would hear the thrum of a nomad's bow, followed by either a roar of approval from the other riders or jeers of derision. Once, at an impossible distance, Zhao saw some kind of large bird fall from the sky seconds after a bow twanged, pierced through the center of its body with a single arrow.

The nomad had shot a bird out of the sky mid-flight.

When the journey finally ended, Zhao felt himself being grasped by rough, strong hands and thrown over a brawny shoulder. He was carried into a felt tent and half-lain, half-thrown onto a smelly straw mat. The bare wooden frame of the tent was visible and there were no furnishings or objects at all inside other than the mat. The ground was the same dry, grassy dirt as outside, and no carpets or rugs covered the floor. The muscular frame of Zhao's carrier left through a flap then re-entered moments later, carrying a wooden bucket and ladle. He dropped the bucket next to Zhao wordlessly and left again.

Zhao had not realized how thirsty he was until he started lapping up water with the ladle, draining the bucket then greedily tipping it back to slurp down what was left after he had gotten all the ladle could reach. His thirst sated, Zhao let himself slip into unconsciousness.

When Zhao awoke, he was parched again. He found his water bucket had been refilled, so he drank deeply. There was a lump of goat cheese sitting on the dirty ground next to the bucket. It was soft and sour, but he devoured it. Zhao was a man of light appetite, but it had been at least a day since he had last eaten, perhaps two. He gulped down two more ladles of water before he felt a powerful need to urinate. When he tried to stand, his body reminded him of his ruined right leg with a renewed wave of pain that had him seeing flashes of light and sent him crashing back down to the mat, gasping desperately.

He attempted to stand on the other side, using only his left leg, but that failed when he bumped his right leg and collapsed again in agony. Eventually Zhao resigned himself to sitting up and using his hand to maneuver his penis around as he urinated so that the urine did not puddle. The dry ground drank up the liquid, but it did not improve the smell inside of the felt tent.

Zhao turned his attention to the condition of his body. He tore away the fabric of his black leggings and looked at his right leg. The skin was broken and the wound had not been washed. Using the remaining water in his bucket, Zhao cleaned the wound and saw one jagged line across his thigh but the cut was not deep. The leg was not twisted or contorted — the fracture appeared to be a simple clean crack in the bone, the delicate tendons and cartilage of the knee had been left undamaged. Breaking sticks off the bare frame of the tent and binding them with the fabric from his torn pant leg, Zhao constructed a makeshift splint to immobilize the leg.

Then he looked at his chest — his armor had been stripped and he was wearing a different shirt, some kind of sleeveless rough-spun woolen shift. Zhao pulled the shift over his head and examined the arrow wounds: two in his right shoulder, one in his chest, the other on his lower left ribs. A fifth wound he could not see was on his back, but those he could see were surrounded by copious crusts of black, dried blood and something else. He touched one wound and found it was coated with something brown and crumbly. He broke a piece off and raised it to his eye, then sniffed it — horseshit, mixed with grass. At least it had stopped him from bleeding out.

Zhao did not appear to be having any trouble breathing, and his urine was not muddied with blood. Those were good signs that no damage had been done to his innards. With time, his leg would heal. More importantly, his captors had taken the time to pull the arrows out of him and patch him up. Granted, they had patched him up with horseshit, but the important thing was that they intended to keep him alive. So long as his wounds did not fester, Zhao's survival was a possibility.

Zhao counted the days by the lumps of cheese he was brought — one fist-sized lump every day. The food churned his stomach and added another dimension of pain to his torturous captivity, but it kept him alive and nourished. The sun appeared to be recently risen when the bulky man came in with a fresh bucket of water and a lump of cheese in his hand. The tent flapping open on his way in and out was the only time Zhao saw light; the thick felt walls of the tent were impermeable to the point that Zhao could not say whether it was day or night at any given time.

The bulky man would drop Zhao's cheese in the dirt and slop the bucket down so that some of the water spilled, as if he regarded feeding and watering Zhao as an extra burden that crowded an already busy morning routine. It seemed he wanted Zhao to know how much he resented having to do it. He never said a word to Zhao, except on the second morning when he saw that Zhao had defecated in the bucket. The bulky man beat Zhao savagely over the head with the bucket and screamed at him in some heavily accented dialect of the Xiongnu language that Zhao did not understand. From then on Zhao crawled on his elbows to the far side of the tent when he needed to defecate and buried his feces in holes he scratched into the dirt with his fingers.

The interior of the tent had grown so putrid by the sixth day that Zhao thought the smell itself might kill him. He wretched and suffered from fever and cold sweats, but the sickness had run its course by the tenth day. He sniffed the wounds he could reach regularly to determine if they were festering and found none of the telltale odors. He was glad of this, until he realized he probably would not be able to detect anything by the smell inside the noxious tent.

It was on the eighteenth day that someone new came into the tent. A squat young man in leather leggings and a dark horsehair vest, whose general appearance was of one slightly too wide and too short, like a distorted image of a man in a bent mirror. His arms were massive, particularly at the bicep where thick veins popped out of sun-darkened skin, and his head sat on an unnaturally bulging pyramid of sloping trapezius muscle rather than a neck. The young man smiled, revealing a mouth full of rot.

"Good hour, you are stopping being bad now," he said in the Xiongnu tongue cheerfully.

Zhao knew the language but had trouble understanding the dialect and did not quite know how to respond, so he said nothing.

"You are stopping being bad now," the young man repeated. Perhaps it was a question.

"My leg is broken, it will take several weeks to heal, but my other wounds are not as bad as they were. Thank you for inquiring." Zhao replied in the Xiongnu language.

"Leg is being fine. You are being good for ride."

Zhao was not sure if this was also a question.

"Pardon, I must beg to differ. I'm not able to ride yet, I'll need more time to heal properly."

The nomad stared at him for a moment.

"Grass in this place is exhausting. We are having to move soon for new pastures. You are riding in four days."

"As you say. I'm your prisoner, I'll cooperate to the best of my ability," Li Zhao said, bowing his head in acquiescence.

"What do you say? Prisoner?" Tone was hard to differentiate in this strange dialect, but Zhao was certain the barbarian sounded shocked and offended.

"Am I not . . . your prisoner?" Zhao asked. Perhaps this nomad was himself a captive of the same chieftain or tribe holding Zhao.

"You are not being prisoner, you are being honored guest!"

Zhao looked at him quizzically. "You believe I am your…guest?"

"Yes! Looking at all we are giving to you." He gestured broadly around the room with one arm. "Giving you delicious cheese every day, giving you great house all to yourself, giving you servant to wait upon all the needs you are having. We are cutting off none of your pieces, no one is making you their wife. How is it you are being prisoner?"

"Pardon, you're . . . mocking, surely? The servant you speak of is a cruel jailor. He beat me with a wooden bucket, the conditions you're keeping me in are squalid, and you're feeding me food that is barely edible and makes me ill."

"Not mocking!" The nomad seemed honestly astonished that Zhao had not recognized his hospitality. He crouched down next to Zhao's mat. "My name is being Mogu. I am great warrior chieftain of this tribe, the Ghuezi."

"No you not! You are little boy who is nothing like his great brother!" A shout came from outside the felt tent.

Mogu stood up and stormed out in a flurry of angry curses that were unfamiliar to Zhao. There were a few sickening thwacks and grunts, then Mogu returned to the tent, his face red and blood on his knuckles.

"Excuse," he said, out of breath. "My name is being Mogu, I am being great warrior chieftain of this tribe, the Ghuezi. You are being attacked by evil bandits from the father-fucking tribe of the Suechian. We are tracking them and then we see they are attacking you." Mogu paused to suck the blood off his knuckles. Zhao could not tell if the blood was his own, or someone else's, or both. "I am seeing your bravery and skill in battle, and I am saying to the Ghuezi, 'There, we save this one. He is great warrior, useful to the Ghuezi.' So now you are living. Because of me."

40

Mogu beamed at Zhao magnanimously, but Zhao did not immediately respond. Mogu simply stared at Zhao expectantly until Zhao realized what he wanted.

"You have my eternal gratitude for your act of great humanity. You are possessed of a benevolent spirit, noble chief Mogu," Zhao intoned solemnly, bowing his head again. "However, in my homeland, there are certain comforts that a guest is customarily offered that differentiate him from a prisoner. If it's not an impertinence, may I make a few small requests? For meals, if you have any rice, I —"

"Yes, yes, yes, just telling your servant what you are needing and he is getting it for you," Mogu interrupted, waving the request away with a hand gesture as if it were an annoying fly.

"Oh, but when I've asked things of him —" Zhao began, but Mogu cut him off again.

"I have more important thing to tell you now, honored guest." Mogu said, his voice growing somber. "Terrible news, I am afraid I am needing to be giving you."

Zhao nodded, signaling Mogu to continue. He had been doing all he could not to think about what had happened to his companions, to Gan Ying. If he allowed himself to despair over Gan Ying's fate, he would not have the strength of spirit he would need to survive captivity.

"In the raid, after you are shot down and trampled I am afraid . . . your horse is being killed." Mogu spoke the words as if they were the most difficult thing he had ever had to tell anyone. He placed a hand on Zhao's shoulder, but appeared unable to make eye contact.

"Pardon. You said my horse was killed?" Zhao asked.

"Yes, I am sorry, honored guest. You need make cry now?"

"No, I think I'll be fine. What of my men? The company of spearmen who were fighting the raiders."

"Oh, yes, all dead too. Some are surrendering and being impaled by the father-fucking tribe of the Suechian." Mogu told Zhao, as if the death and torture of the soldiers were a mildly interesting afterthought to the real tragedy, which had been the death of the horse.

Zhao cringed. He had expected that his men had been killed. He had only been marching with that particular company for a year and a half, and as a commanding officer he could never get too emotionally attached to his troops. It was still difficult to hear. And the impalement of some of them made it even worse. That was a slow, horrible death.

"And the others?" Zhao asked. "The mounted men? There was one among them whose name was Gan Ying. He was a Chinese general, an envoy of the Son of Heaven and the Protector General Ban Chao. Do you know what happened to him? Was he killed too?"

"You are wanting to find this man, Ganging?" Mogu sounded curious.

"Yes, very much."

"Oh, well, he is being captured. All of the Han riders are. The father-fucking tribe of the Suechian saw they are wearing robes of readers so they are bringing them back. Han readers are being very useful. I am seeing the father-fucking Suechian take these men captive myself, definitely intending to be keeping them and using them, definitely."

Zhao felt a flood of relief — Gan Ying lived! Zhao's mission still had a possibility of being fulfilled. He laughed out loud and slapped the ground.

"This is great news!" Zhao declared. "Tell me, Mogu, can the Ghuezi defeat the Suechian in battle? How many men do you have riding for you?"

"The Ghuezi was once being a great warrior band! For the Ghuezi, four hundred and twenty men of fighting age were once riding," he said.

"And how many currently?"

Mogu looked down at the dirt. "Not so many, I think."

"Do you know how many?" Zhao pressed.

"Maybe eighty," Mogu said. "When Mogu's brother, Khaku, was chief, everybody being happy. But then Khaku is dying and Mogu is becoming chief. Everyone says Mogu is being too young to be chief. Mogu is not having been in any battles. So the best warriors are leaving to join the father-fucking tribe of the Suechian. Now only the young and the old and the women and the injured stay in the Ghuezi. All the others are having left."

Mogu's shame was so palpable that Li Zhao felt a swelling of sympathy for him.

"And the Suechian? How many warriors can they field?" Zhao asked.

"The father-fucking tribe of the Suechian is having six hundred and ninety fighting men, I think," Mogu said.

"Would it be accurate to say that relations between the Ghuezi and the filially-philandering tribe of the Suechian are hostile?" Zhao asked.

"The Ghuezi hates the father-fucking tribe of the Suechian!" Mogu shouted. He leapt to his feet and began pacing. "They are always raiding us and stealing our best horses and our best goats! They are taking the beautiful women and leaving only the old and the ugly. They are burning our tents and raiding the caravans we are wanting to raid." Mogu kicked at the dirt as if he were kicking a tiny member of the Suechian. "But then the Ghuezi are finding you. My father and my brother are riding in the wars between the Han and the Xiongnu. The Xiongnu are having huge armies, bigger than those of the Han, but the Han are winning. Using tricks. Poisoning water, burning crops. My father and brother are telling me that this is dishonorable. Sneaky. But I am always thinking this is better way to fight."

Zhao nodded. "Sun Tzu said to attack by stratagem."

"Yes! Attacking by stratagem. That is what we are needing to do. And you are Han. You can make stratagems because you are being of a dishonorable and sneaky people."

Mogu did not say this with malice, so Zhao let it pass without objection.

"So what are you saying, honored guest?" Mogu asked, crouching down and grinning at Zhao, excitement in his eyes. "We are working together, defeating the father-fucking tribe of the Suechian, and rescuing your Ganging, yes?"

Zhao paused for a moment. This young chieftain seemed sincere, but he was still a barbarian. He had imprisoned Zhao for many days, inflicted great hardship upon him. Did Zhao really want to aid his captor?

Mogu sensed his hesitation.

"Or, if you are not wanting to help, we are driving a stake under your ribcage and leaving you impaled on the plains to die slowly as the wolves and vultures tear at your flesh."

"I will gladly render the mighty Ghuezi my services, noble chief Mogu," Zhao said, as quickly as he could.

At Zhao's request, Mogu gave Zhao a pair of wooden staffs with their ends wrapped in felt. Using these as crutches and with a more secure splint for his leg, Zhao was able to move around the campsite of the Ghuezi. The landscape of relatively flat grassland stretched for as far as the eye could see in every direction except north, where Zhao could make out a mountain range in the distance. Spaced widely apart in no particular pattern were about three dozen round felt tents with domed tops, all of them identical in size and color.

Goats, sheep, horses, and dogs wandered just as freely as the people amongst the tents, each individual nomad corralling his or her own little herd of animals from horseback. Many more horses, goats, and sheep grazed in the lands surrounding the tent town. In fact, people seemed to be outnumbered at least five to one by animals in this community.

Most remarkable to Zhao was the fact that everyone was mounted almost all the time. Not just the men of fighting age, but the women too. Even children rode. Zhao saw a child who could not have been more than three years old, sitting a horse more comfortably than Zhao ever had. No wonder the Xiongnu produced such marvelous cavalry — this lifeway had made horsemanship such a central component that a nomad was more comfortable mounted than on foot. Indeed, Zhao noticed Mogu and the others were all somewhat bow-legged when they did dismount, as if their hips were not used to being unsupported by the broad back of a horse.

Most of the people of the tribe spent the day herding their goats and horses as they grazed the surrounding grasslands, and some of the men went off to hunt or scout for trading caravans to raid. When the sheep were shorn, their wool was beaten into felt or spun, and this task was one usually performed by the women and the children, but other than that there appeared to be no real distinction between the duties of the men and those of the women. Women spent as much time herding as men and a few of the younger, fitter women even joined the raiding and hunting parties. The women wore the same simple clothes as the men: leggings or trousers made from leather, shirts and shifts made from horsehair or rough spun wool.

Mogu often invited Zhao to join the herding and raiding parties, but Zhao always had to remind Mogu that he could not ride because of his broken leg. It seemed that Mogu had a difficult time understanding the concept of someone not being able to ride. But now that his crutches gave him some limited means of getting around, Zhao began taking evening meals with Mogu and a large group of the younger members of the Ghuezi around a fire.

"Here, you are drinking this, honored guest," Mogu said to Zhao during one such meal while handing him a horse skin satchel containing a pulpy, foul-smelling white liquid.

"What is it?" Zhao asked. He had just choked down a plateful of particularly tough roasted antelope and was not sure his stomach would be able to handle any more of the harsh foods that the nomads prized.

"Kumis. Is making you very strong," Mogu said. He had been taking frequent swigs from the satchel all evening, and it had given his cheeks the rosy red flush normally associated with drinking rice wine.

Zhao hesitated as he brought the bag to his lips — all the nomads around the fire were watching him expectantly. He swilled it back and his mouth was filled with the most awful flavor he had ever tasted. It was creamy and bitter, like liquid moldy cheese and ash, and little pieces of horsehair from the bag floated around in the liquid. Zhao spewed it out and the tribe erupted in laughter. Mogu's huge, freakishly muscular hand slammed his back as Zhao repeatedly spat, trying to get as much of the foul-tasting drink out of his mouth as he could.

"Is being too strong for you, I am thinking!" Mogu declared, grabbing the bag back and taking a huge swill himself.

"Pardon, I didn't mean to waste your drink," Zhao said, once he had recovered.

"Is no waste! Is making whole tribe laugh."

"I'm glad you're amused. What's it made of?"

"Kumis is fermented milk of the mare," a young woman named Bulga seated on the other side of Mogu said to Zhao, taking a deep swig herself. She made only the slightest of faces before passing the bag along.

"I see. I don't suppose you might have acquired any tea or rice wine on your recent caravan raids, have you?" Zhao asked.

Mogu waved his hand, indicating no. Zhao had noted this habit: the Ghuezi waved their hands for no. In his experience, every people had their own way of communicating with gestures as idiosyncratic as their language and dialect. The only exception Zhao had found was the nod which, as a sort of modified bow, was a universal signal of acquiescence or a substitute for the word 'yes.'

"I didn't think so. Perhaps when we make our attack on the Suechian some other beverages will be among the spoils. Have we gathered any intelligence on their position yet?" Zhao asked, his question directed to the assembled young men and women of the tribe as much as to Mogu.

A few of the members of the tribe waved no's, but most were silent.

"How is it you are wanting to attack the father-fucking tribe of the Suechian anyway, Han man?" Bulga asked. "They are outnumbering us six to one. We are not having any chance of defeating them."

"Sun Tzu said, 'He will win who knows how to handle both superior and inferior forces,'" Zhao replied. "I have a stratagem in mind. We can win, but we have to be fierce and intelligent."

"None are fiercer in battle than the mighty Ghuezi!" One of the young men declared.

"The Suechian are," a wrinkled old man said. "I am having fought in forty-seven great battles. Many of the tribes I am riding with are fiercer in battle than the Ghuezi. You only say this because you are being young and foolish, Kulug."

The young man, Kulug, stood up, fists clenched, to challenge the older man. "You are who is being foolish, Gatu! You are weak but the Ghuezi are not!"

Gatu rose to meet Kulug's challenge but Mogu stood as well.

"Both of you are sitting now!" Mogu shouted.

Kulug did not break his stare from the older Gatu, and Gatu waved Mogu's order away. They both backed out from the circle around the fire and Gatu struck Kulug in the face with a closed fist. Kulug absorbed the blow and tackled Gatu to the ground, where the two began to wrestle. Mogu shouted for them to stop but they both ignored him. Gatu appeared to be losing the wrestling match to the younger, stronger Kulug, when he all of a sudden he slipped out from under Kulug's arm and slithered his legs and arms around Kulug's, gripping him in an inescapable hold. Kulug tried to tap out but the wizened old Gatu refused to let go.

"Releasing him, Gatu," Mogu ordered, but Gatu's face was flushed with drunkenness and anger.

Mogu stormed over to Gatu and hooked two fingers in his inner cheek. With this fishhook grip, he jerked Gatu off and began savagely kicking the old man, who curled up defensively but did not fight back.

"I am leader of the Ghuezi, Gatu! When I am telling you to do something, you are doing it!"

Then Mogu turned his attention to Kulug, who was sitting on the ground nursing a sore shoulder.

"Are you being alright, Kulug?"

Kulug nodded.

"Good."

Mogu proceeded to punch Kulug in the face, quickly, three times.

Mogu wiped off his bloody knuckles on his pant leg and resumed his seat next to Zhao.

"The Ghuezi will be fierce in battle, honored guest," Mogu assured Zhao, picking up the conversation as if the altercation had not even occurred. "But how are you to lead us if you do not ride?"

"I'll endure anything to defeat the Suechian, to rescue my master Gan Ying, and to restore the honor of the Ghuezi," Zhao said, rising to his feet. He spoke in the same sonorous tones he employed when addressing soldiers before battle. The Ghuezi were demoralized and divided, they needed inspiration if they were going to be of any use to him. "Tomorrow, I'll ride out with a party of scouts to find the Suechian myself. Once we've determined their location, we'll return in force, and the Ghuezi will defeat their enemy once and for all!

CHAPTER FOUR

Mogu and Zhao set out on their mission early the next morning with a group of five riders for support. Mogu leant Zhao one of his own mares. Although the mare was shorter and shaggier than the horses he was used to, her head was large and her chest was deep and stocky. She looked strong and healthy, with a long mane and an extraordinarily long tail with fawn-coloring that faded into black legs.

Zhao limped up behind the horse that Mogu had pointed out to him, his leg still splinted but his crutches now discarded, carrying a saddle in both arms. Zhao slung the saddle across the back of the horse, but she darted forward and whinnied the moment the saddle touched her back. Zhao lost his balance and stumbled backwards.

"What are you doing? That is not how you are approaching horse!" Mogu shouted at Zhao. "Are you knowing nothing? Here, letting me show."

Mogu walked forward, slowly, to the shaggy little mare, with his hand outstretched, making cooing noises. Seeing her human, she calmed slightly, and then relaxed more as Mogu stroked her head and whispered to her.

"She is not a tool for using. She is a free being, you must persuade her.

You must calming her, talking to her, getting her permission before just dropping saddle on her back. You must be approaching from the front, at angle. Not directly from the front, avoiding her blind spot, and never ever from behind."

"I see," Zhao said, watching carefully as Mogu cooed to the mare. She seemed completely calm now and Mogu indicated for Zhao to come forward.

"Never forgetting, horses are prey animal. Like deer or antelope. Not like dog, who is predator animal. Instincts are being very different for prey and for predator. Always remembering this when dealing with horses, yes? They are being scared very easily."

"Yes, that makes sense," Zhao nodded.

"Now you are trying," Mogu ordered. "Being very nice, using softest voice, asking and not telling."

"Hello, sweet friend," Zhao said, doing his best to mimic Mogu's lilting tone. "Hello, good horse. You're a beautiful creature."

He stared into her big, brown, glassy eyes, hypnotized somewhat, and reached out to stroke her. She whinnied slightly and backed up.

"Not looking into eyes, this is being intimidating!" Mogu said. "And moving hand slowly. Approaching slowly. Doing all things slowly. Remember, they are being prey. Easily startled."

Zhao tried again, and failed again. Everything he did in some way startled the poor horse. These steppe horses were deeply bonded with their owners and thus were reluctant to be ridden by someone new. Zhao had always thought of horses as beasts of burden but the Ghuezi treated them like pets or even children.

"Looking at silly Han man!" Bulga jeered as Zhao struggled with the process. "Says he is attacking the father fucking Suechian, but he is struggling with horse like baby!"

Zhao's felt his face redden as Bulga and the others laughed. He took a deep breath, calmed his mind. The Ghuezi did everything on horseback: fighting, herding, hunting, traveling, they even a practiced a strange type of mounted arm-wrestling for sport. To them, a warrior who could not ride was as much of a contradiction as an illiterate scholar.

When Zhao finally mounted the mare, Mogu gave a loud whistle and his own horse trotted up. It waited patiently beside him as obediently as a well-trained dog. Zhao had no idea, previously, that horses could be trained in such a way. Mogu slipped one leg into a leather stirrup that hung from the saddle and leaped across the horse's back in a single bound. Mogu's horse took up a brisk trot, his retainers and Zhao followed after him. A half dozen shaggy dogs followed behind.

They rode northwest, towards the distant Tian Shan mountain range, in the direction that the Suechian were last seen. They rode at a much faster pace than Zhao had ever ridden before, galloping for long stretches without resting.

"We are having much ground to cover," Mogu explained when Zhao asked why they were riding so hard. "The herds of the father-fucking tribe of the Suechian are being much bigger and exhausting their pastures sooner, so they are moving more often and further than the Ghuezi. They are moving long distances in the time since you are attacked, we must travel fast to be catching them."

"But what about the horses?" Zhao asked. "They can't keep galloping forever."

Mogu laughed. "Steppe horses are being much stronger than your weak Han horses, honored guest," he said, slapping his own horses flank. "Bones are being stronger because soil here is being better. Weak Han soil is breeding weak grass, weak grass is breeding weak horses. This is why the Han are having to ride into battle in silly little carts or fight on foot."

Zhao fought the desire to correct Mogu on the point that a war chariot was a far cry from a 'silly little cart,' but he knew he had a point. The first of the Han-Xiongnu wars had been fought by the Martial Emperor, in part over access to the steppe horses, and, just as importantly, the grass seeds that would sustain them. Zhao could feel the sturdiness of his mount between his legs in contrast to the thin, taller horse he had ridden briefly during the Suechian raid. This horse was strong, stocky, and completely unburdened by his weight.

"The last thing my master Gan Ying said to me before we were attacked was how poor he thought the soil here was," Zhao said. "He said it was inferior to Chinese soil because it can't be cultivated to grow millet."

Mogu laughed heartily and patted his own horse. "Tell Ganging to meet me in battle riding a bowl of millet porridge while I am riding a horse of the steppe and we shall see whose soil is superior!"

Zhao laughed as well. "Excellent point, my friend."

As they rode that day, Bulga noticed a grazing ibex. A great male, larger than any domestic goat Zhao had ever seen, with ribbed horns half the length of its body that curled back into wicked points. Like a dog that had sighted a rabbit, Bulga's whole body tensed when she laid eyes on the creature and she held up her hands to halt the other riders. Mogu and Khaku both reached for their bows, but Bulga stopped them with a snarl. She slid four arrows out of the quiver on her saddlebag. Holding three of them in her bow hand, she strung the fourth and set her horse to a slow, delicate walk in the direction of the unsuspecting creature.

When its head twitched, Bulga shouted a 'ky-ah' and her horse burst into a gallop. The ibex darted away, but its great advantage was in its ability to scale hills and mountainsides, and it had strayed far from the safety of its home in Tian Shan Mountains to the north. Here in the flat grasslands between the mountains and the desert, the creature was outmatched by the speed of Bulga's horse, which rapidly closed the distance between the ibex and the huntress.

Bulga stood in her leather stirrups and set loose an arrow at full gallop that hit the ibex in its flank. It stumbled and Bulga put two more arrows in it, one more to the flank and the other in its ribs. She fired the fourth arrow from close range into the back of its neck. The ibex was on its side, kicking and twitching. Zhao saw Bulga dismount and rush to the creature, cutting its throat quickly with a knife and holding its head while it bled out. As Zhao and the others approached, he saw her staring into the creature's big, wide eyes and heard her saying something in soft tones that he could not quite make out.

When Bulga stood, she sniffed and wiped her eyes with the back of her left hand — cupped in her right hand was a puddle of the ibex' blood. She did not acknowledge the others yet and they said nothing to her. Slowly, reverently, looking up at the sky, Bulga smeared the blood on her face.

"Tengri!" She shouted at the sky, holding her arms open. "Thanking you for this gift! We are making good use of him."

The other nomads tilted their heads back for a moment as well, looking up at the blue sky above them. Zhao did the same. When the moment passed, the nomads all congratulated Bulga on her kill, leaning over from their horses to pat her on the back and admire the size of its horns and the amount of muscle on its legs. She grinned through the blood on her face as she basked in their thanks and congratulations. She glanced at Zhao, but looked away before he could offer any kind words of his own. Bulga was young, no more than nineteen or twenty, and one of the only young women not taken from the Ghuezi by Suechian raiders. She seemed eager to be accepted by the other warriors, Zhao thought, probably because she felt out of place in a tribe where she had no one of her own age and gender. Bringing down the great ibex had clearly won her some of that acceptance.

They made camp early that evening to have time to cook the fresh meat. The group of seven was traveling lightly and each rider was tailed by one remount, except for Zhao and Mogu: Mogu brought three remounts and Zhao had none. The remounts were all lightly laden with supplies, including the props and cover of a felt tent. Working as a team to erect the frame of the tent, the six nomads had the round building up and anchored securely within minutes, each of them running through the routine of hammering down the shorter outer poles and the longer central pole, running the lattice along the sides, and layering the thick, dense strips of felt over the frame as if they had done it a thousand times. Zhao initially attempted to help, but he soon found he was just getting in the way, so he stepped back and let the nomads work.

They spit roasted a large chunk of ibex meat over a fire that evening and packed the rest in salt. Bulga had borrowed an iron handsaw from Kulug and shorn the huge horns off the head of the ibex. Temperatures dropped fast at night in the grasslands, but the shaggy horses were kept warm by their coats and the felt walls of the tent were remarkably effective at keeping the heat in. They ate the roasted ibex meat and passed around a skin of foul-smelling kumis. Zhao passed on the kumis as did Bulga, who was busy hacking away at the severed horns of the ibex with her borrowed handsaw, slicing the tough horn into long, thin strips. Once everyone was full, and everyone except Zhao and Bulga were drunk, they all fell asleep on straw mats.

The next morning the party broke camp and set out at dawn. The dogs had fallen behind the previous day but had caught up in the evening and were found snuggled together outside the felt tent. The humans fed the dogs and ate leftover roasted ibex meat before setting off, but by midafternoon Zhao was growing hungry again. He had spent the past several weeks lying on a straw mat and doing little exercise, so riding all day was taking more out of him than he had anticipated.

"Mogu!" Zhao shouted over the noise of hooves beating the dry ground. "Do we have any extra food?"

Mogu looked at Zhao quizzically. "If you are hungering, just borrowing some life from your horse."

Mogu had said this as if it were the most obvious thing in the world, but Zhao did not quite know what to make of it.

"What do you mean 'borrow some life from my horse?'"

"Here, I am showing you."

Mogu drew a small knife from his belt and ran his thumb across the back of his horse's neck, as if searching for something. When he found the feature he was looking for, he made a tiny slice in the skin with the knife, no longer than his thumbnail, but a surprisingly profuse a trickle of blood appeared. Mogu wrapped his mouth around the cut and sucked enthusiastically, like a babe at the teat. He pulled away after about fifteen seconds and grinned at Zhao, his teeth, lips and chin dripping red.

"You are trying now!" Mogu said.

"Oh, um, no, that's fine, I'm really not all that hungry after all," Zhao said, thinking that he would rather drink a whole skin of kumis than suck blood from the back of a horse's neck.

They fell into a regular routine of riding all day, making camp, eating and sleeping, then waking up again and riding. For an hour or so before bed every evening, Bulga would work on her horn construct. After she had finished the project of cutting the ibex horn into long, thin strips, she began boiling sinew and cartilage from the same beast in a little pot over a fire she tended outside of the tent while the others drank kumis and made idle conversation. Zhao wondered exactly what it was that she was doing with all of these odd animal parts but no one seemed to question her and he decided to leave her to her own affairs.

"Mogu, why are you so sure the Suechian won't have killed my master?" Zhao asked Mogu once the tent had been erected and Bulga had begun tending her little pot of boiling animal tissue. "You said that they value Han scholars, but I've been living with you for weeks now and I haven't seen any way they could be of use. Gan Ying and the others are experts in philosophy, literature, mathematics, even logistics and bureaucracy, but out here it's horsemanship and archery that matter, not education or literacy."

It was a question that had been festering in Zhao's mind for days. It was possible that the Suechian might have preserved Gan Ying's life once they realized he had been sent by Protector General Ban Chao. As the man who had crushed the Kangju, the Xiongnu, and the Kushans, he was feared by the steppe nomads like no other Chinese man had ever been. It was more likely, however, that Gan Ying and the others had simply been killed and stripped of all their treasure.

"Readers are being very valuable to steppe people," Mogu assured him. "They are being used for trading in cities. The father-fucking tribe of the Suechian might be capturing a merchant caravan with one hundred bolts of silk, but what are they doing with one hundred bolts of silk? Are they living in silk tents? Dressing their horses in silk?" He laughed. "Maybe it is nice to be wearing silk, yes, but there are being more important things. So the tribe is taking silk to cities. Qiuci, Kashgar, Karashar, Aksu, Urumqi, places like this. In the great oasis cities, tribes can be trading silk for more useful things. Salt for preserving of food. Iron arrowheads and swords and armor. Birch for tent frames and arrow shafts."

Zhao realized this was true. He had seen only occasional tamarisk trees since leaving Qiuci and certainly no forests, yet the Ghuezi used plenty of wood. The Ghuezi had no foundries or blacksmiths but had plenty of iron tools. Even their sparse lifestyle that seemed, on its surface, to be self-sufficient relied heavily on trade.

"But in these trading cities, merchants know that we cannot read their marks," Mogu continued. "They are telling us the contract we are agreeing to is saying one thing, but it is really saying another. Then they are cheating us on the deal, but the magistrates are saying that the deal was what the marks said and not what the man said! The readers are helping with this, being good for trading."

"That seems like such a waste, though," Zhao said. "For them to capture a great general, an imperial envoy, only to have him haggle over the price of stolen silks."

Mogu waved the objection away. "Maybe it is seeming like a waste to you, but it is making a big difference for us."

"They could just as easily kidnap a common merchant, and there are certainly no shortage of them to be found on these trade routes," Zhao said. "What I want to know is why Gan Ying? What makes him so much more valuable to the Suechian?"

Mogu began to respond, but at that moment Bulga walked in, carrying her little pot of melted sinew and cartilage. The pot was still piping hot and she handled it carefully with thick horsehair gloves. Zhao saw that the sinew and cartilage had completely dissolved into a gooey, translucent, and greenish-yellow paste.

"Fetch me my pack, Han man," Bulga said to Zhao, without looking at him.

"Of course," Zhao said. He ran out to her black gelding and returned with a horse skin bag, which Bulga snatched from him wordlessly.

From the bag, Bulga pulled the strips of horn she had been carving. She also took out strips of birch wood, roughly equal in width and thickness to the horn strips, and a bundle of horsehair twine. Bulga slathered the paste onto the horn and birch strips, using it as glue to bind them together and supporting the glue with the horsehair twine. The only light in the tent was from the fire outside the open tent flap, but Bulga's slim, gnarled fingers moved quickly, piecing together the strips into a long, loose D-shape with such practiced efficiency that Zhao thought she might have been able to do it in total darkness. The bone thumb ring on her right hand glinted in the light as she worked. Bulga stayed up long after the others had all fallen asleep, apparently intent on finishing the project that night, and Zhao lost himself watching her, admiring her skill and dexterity.

"Why are you watching me, Han man?" She barked at Zhao, never quite taking her eyes off her task.

"Pardon, I didn't mean to cause distraction," Zhao said, turning away.

"Am I saying you are distracting? No. I am asking why you are watching me. Are you wanting to take me as a wife?"

"Oh, pardon, no. I'm sorry, no, that's not what I was thinking. No, pardon."

"Why not?"

"Oh, I . . . um . . ."

57

"Because I am not being delicate little painted Han princess, you are not thinking I am being a good wife? I am having killed fourteen different men and having had only six different cocks. A woman who has taken more lives than cocks is very rare, many men are wanting to have her."

"Oh, of course, of course. I didn't mean to imply otherwise. You're indeed a . . . beautiful and desirable woman, according to the custom of your people," Zhao said, saving his honesty with the qualification.

Bulga was not hideous, but her face was squashed and her body was broad, much like Mogu's. She had the gnarled, unclean look of all barbarians with grit and dirt worked deep into her pores. She dressed like any of the men, in a shapeless woolen shift that concealed her form. It was only her hairless cheeks and voice that betrayed her gender.

"All I meant to say was I wasn't watching you out of any carnal desire, but out of admiration for your . . . your . . ."

"My what?"

"Pardon, I do not know the word for it in your tongue. In my language, we call it *'gongfu.'* It means excellent skill, acquired through hard work and deliberate practice."

Bulga paused.

"I think we are not having a word for this."

"But you do have it," Zhao told her.

Zhao's groin and thighs ached from riding so much, and the skin on his inner legs was chafed badly. After a week and a half in the saddle, though, Zhao had gotten used to the discomforts. Kulug had even given him some kind of foul-smelling ointment that did wonders for chafing. His broken right leg had mostly healed in the weeks since the attack and he no longer used the splint. It was weak, but he exercised it with squats and wushu forms every evening and every morning.

They were getting close to the Suechian, Mogu insisted. He said he could tell by the grass. To Zhao, the grass all looked the same, but Mogu claimed that the grass they were riding over had recently been grazed upon, although he could not explain exactly what made this so obvious to him. The only changes Zhao could identify were that the rolling plains and gentle hills of the grassland had given way to larger grassy hills and even the occasional steep cliff.

Mogu did manage to explain to Zhao exactly how the Xiongnu horsemen were able to fire arrows accurately at full gallop, though. This was something Zhao had been wondering about since the Suechian had attacked his party. He had, of course, seen many Xiongnu fire at a gallop in battle, but when tens of thousands of men are firing at once, accuracy is neither necessary nor noticeable. It was not until he saw the cavalry archers in a small group that he was able to understand the extent of each individual warrior's skill.

"The moment all four of the horses hooves are being off the ground is the moment you are releasing the arrow," Mogu told Zhao. "You must be breathing out as you release, letting go of the arrow as you are letting go of your breath. There must be nothing that can be shaking your aim."

Zhao found that this secret technique was more easily explained than performed. Borrowing Mogu's bow, for he had lost his in the raid, Zhao urged his mare to a gallop and practiced shooting arrows at a small target on the heavy felt walls of the tent, waiting for the exact moment in her gait when she was completely off the ground, but always missing both the moment and the target. After the felt walls of the tent were peppered with arrows, none of them in the target, Zhao grew frustrated and returned the bow to Mogu.

"It's a difficult skill to master," Zhao said. "I don't appear to have the patience for it."

"You need to be getting patience, Han man," barked Bulga from behind him. "You are having your own bow now. Like a real warrior."

"Pardon?"

"Here, is finished setting. For you."

Bulga was on foot, holding the long, D-shaped construct of bone and wood, the horsehair twine ties removed. She knelt down and instructed one of the other riders to help her. Bulga bent the construct over her knee against the curve, while the other rider passed a long thread through one end and tied it to the other. Now it was M-shaped and its purpose was clear — it was a composite bow, the signature weapon of the nomadic warrior.

"It's wonderful," Zhao said, taking the bow in his hand and admiring it. He plucked the string and heard a thrum, then pulled the string all the way back. "Incredible. Bending it against the natural curve adds so much power. And it's so light! It might be a better bow than yours, Mogu."

Mogu grunted and Bulga gave her chief a snide smile.

"Thank you, Bulga," Zhao said. "This is one of the greatest gifts I've ever received. I'll treasure it for the rest of my days."

Bulga opened her mouth, but Zhao never heard what she intended to say. Because right at that moment, an arrow buzzed across her neck.

The arrow continued past her, its flight uninterrupted as if it had only grazed her throat, and stuck in the wall of the felt tent. For a moment, all was still. A thin red line appeared on Bulga's neck — it beaded, then grew thicker. Bulga's expression was of confusion, and her hands went up to her neck, as if to hold it together. But within seconds, a waterfall of blood was gushing through her fingers.

"No!" Zhao cried. He lurched towards Bulga, even as he realized she was beyond saving. Her knees gave out beneath her and the color drained from her face, but her hands never stopped trying to close the hole across her throat.

"Suechian father-fuckers!" Mogu roared, and urged his mount over the hillock in the direction from which the arrow had been fired.

More arrows were buzzing in the direction of Zhao and Bulga, and within moments the nomad who had helped Bulga string the bow was so full of arrows he looked like a human pincushion. Zhao shouted for Mogu to return, but Mogu had already whirled in retreat by the time Zhao's mouth had opened.

"Go, go, go!" Mogu yelled.

From behind the hillock, arrows arced towards Mogu, some missing him and his horse by inches. Kulug and the others mounted and were off. At his whistle, the remaining horses galloped after Mogu. Zhao turned in the saddle and saw a cadre of mounted warriors charging after them. Arrows fell right behind them, but their horses were no faster than those of the Ghuezi, so Zhao and the others were able to stay just on the edge of their range. The bodies of Bulga and the other nomad were trampled by the attacking horde. Mogu's dogs tried desperately to keep up with their master, but they had no hope of outrunning galloping horses. Zhao heard high-pitched whines as the dogs, too, were trampled. The felt tent was abandoned and Kulug was struck with an arrow in the back of the neck. He died in the saddle, but his gelding kept pace with the rest of the Ghuezi.

The chase lasted for hours, but the rate of fire slowed as the Suechian ran out of arrows. No one else was killed. When the sun was low in the sky, the Suechian peeled off.

"They must be noticing us scouting them," Mogu said, breaking a long silence. "Sending raiders out to scare us off."

"That was overkill to chase off scouts," Zhao said. "There were at least a hundred men in that party. Is there something you aren't telling me about them, Mogu? I can't plan a strategy if you keep information from me."

Mogu waved a no but Zhao remained skeptical.

The ride back was much, much harder. They slept in their saddles, stuffing grass under their clothes and hugging their shaggy horses for warmth. Mogu lamented the loss of his favorite dog. Zhao thought about

Bulga's face as she died. She was a strange woman: hard and tough, as one had to be in the grasslands. Yet, she was also sweet and generous — confident and dead.

Bulga was dead because of the father-fucking Suechian.

"Mogu might be hiding something about them," Zhao told himself, "but whatever it is, it can't justify her murder. I'll see to it that you're avenged, Bulga. I promise."

CHAPTER FIVE

"Collect as much grass as you can," Zhao instructed the assembled group of children back at the Ghuezi campsite. "Just go out to the north and pile it into water buckets, then bundle it with horsehair twine. Leave the bundles out to dry. I want as many dry bundles as you can gather in the next few days. Make sure each bundle is at least this thick," he said, indicating the width of his arm.

"I need felt, lots of it. If there are any sheep that can be shorn, do it today," he told the old women. "The rest will have to come from the tents. For the next few nights, we'll need to sleep double. That'll free up half our tent felt for use in the battle. And if anyone has anything else — blankets, cloaks, shifts, even hats — please consider donating it. If we defeat the Suechian, you'll have your pick of the loot to replace what you give."

"And what if you are losing in battle to the father-fucking Suechian?" a toothless old woman wanted to know.

"Then we are all dying and the father-fucking tribe of the Suechian are taking the young women as wives and impaling the old, ugly women like you on stakes," Mogu barked back at her. "Either way, you are needing to give to the honored guest your felts."

The old woman acquiesced, grumbling, as did the others.

"I need you to take whatever wood you can and carve spears," Zhao told the assembled group of young men and women. "Use arrowheads for the spear tips. Use tent poles or find tamarisk trees to cut down. And once you have enough spears, nail them together with crossbeams so that they form a sort of fence, like so."

Zhao demonstrated what he meant by making a crosshatch pattern with his fingers.

"It doesn't have to be perfect," Zhao told them. "The spears only have to be roughly equal length, but it's very important that they're nailed together securely. I need as many spears as you can make, crafted into two long fences, the longer the better."

"This should being done by slaves, not warriors!" one of the young men protested. "I am being a free man of the Ghuezi! I am riding. I am hunting. I am herding. I am raiding. I am fighting. I am not building like a Han slave."

"Where are all your slaves being?" Mogu asked the young man, making a show of looking around. "Oh, yes, you are not having slaves! So you are doing this yourself. Maybe after the battle when we are making the father-fucking tribe of the Suechian our slaves, then you are using slaves to do things for you, but until then you are doing as you are told!"

Mogu cuffed him across the ear to drive home the point. The young man was sullen but did not protest further.

"Noble chief Mogu, I beg your pardon if I'm being insolent, but I need to ask you something," Zhao said, once he was alone with Mogu. "Do all the nomadic chiefs treat their people like you do?"

"What are you meaning?" Mogu asked.

"I mean, when you hear objections from your tribe, you lash back. It's as if you take every question or opinion as a personal challenge, and you're so quick to use violence."

"This is what a chief is supposed to be. He is telling the tribe what to do and they are doing it. If they are not doing it, he is punishing them."

"So there's no concept of reciprocal obligation in your political philosophy? With due respect, you're ruling your tribe more like Emperor Qin Shi Huangdi than Emperor Gaozu of Han."

"I am not knowing what you are talking about."

"Pardon. Qin Shi Huang founded the Qin Dynasty and reunited the Middle Kingdom after the long Warring States period. He believed what you just said, that a ruler is entitled to obedience and disobedience should be punished harshly. That was the essence of his philosophy, legalism."

"I am liking this legalism," Mogu said.

"I thought you would, but the Qin Dynasty only barely outlived its founder," Zhao said. "Because the people rebelled against those harsh laws and, after a period of war, Emperor Gaozu established the Han Dynasty. The Han Dynasty has survived for hundreds of years because it took a different philosophy, mitigating the harshness of legalism with the morality of Confucianism."

"So? Steppe peoples are not soft like Han peoples."

Zhao sighed. Perhaps lessons drawn from Sima Qian's Records of the Grand Historian did not feel as pertinent to Mogu as they did to Zhao. They were too distant, too alien. He needed a more immediate example. "May I ask, how did your late brother, Khaku, treat the tribe? Was he as strict as you?"

"What?" Mogu whirled on Zhao, his mood suddenly changed, tension filling his bulging trapezius muscles. "Why are you talking about Khaku? What is he being to you?"

"Pardon, I didn't mean to bring up any memories that cause you grief," Zhao said, holding up his hands, unsure if grief could explain such a reaction. "I only meant that your tribe seems to have loved Khaku. Maybe reflecting on why they did could help you become a better chief."

"Are you saying I am not being a good chief?" Mogu asked, leering at Zhao.

"I think you're trying to be the best chief you can be," Zhao said, "but I do have some limited knowledge of political philosophy that might help you become even better."

Mogu said nothing but looked at Zhao expectantly. Zhao took this as permission to continue.

"You need to establish your authority over your tribe, yes. Occasionally you'll need to use force, but you have to temper that with kindness. The essence of Confucian political philosophy is that the relationship between ruler and subject is governed by the same principles as the relationship between father and son, master and student, husband and wife, older and younger friend. It's all about reciprocal obligation." Zhao gestured out at the tribe, who were working on preparing the felts, the spears, and the grass bundles. "You don't demand their obedience at the point of your sword, you offer your benevolence in exchange for it."

Mogu was silent for a moment. "How am I doing this?" he asked.

Zhao smiled. "You once told me, 'asking, not telling.' That seems like as good a rule for people as it is for horses."

Mogu grunted and nodded, looking off into the distance. Zhao couldn't be sure, but he felt like he had gotten through to the chief.

Zhao, when not supervising or participating in the battle preparations, rode his borrowed mare out from the camp over a hillock and practiced his horseback archery. He began to practice deliberately, breaking the action of firing at a gallop down into its constituent parts, just like he had been taught to do with all aspects of combat in the southern monastery where he had trained many years ago.

The first part was identifying the correct moment to fire. He practiced galloping on the shaggy mare with no bow in his hands. He simply said the word 'release' whenever he felt her leave the ground and the word 'bump' with each couple of footfalls.

It was not about finding the right moment, he soon realized. It was about finding the rhythm of her gallop. He refocused and attuned himself to her, thinking of her body as an extension of his own. Once he did that, aligning his words to her rhythm became easy.

Then he added in the bow, but without any arrows. Again he chanted, but this time he plucked the empty bowstring with every 'release.'

The rhythm was so natural after a short time. Now he added a distant felt target and arrows. The first bump was the moment to draw the arrow; the second bump was to notch it and pull back.

He loosed twelve arrows in about a minute, all but two were on target. It was a level of accuracy and rate of fire that any nomadic horseman would be proud of.

The day of the battle had arrived. Li Zhao had repaired and polished his armor, replacing the punctured iron scales with new ones made from hammered arrowheads. Instead of the shin-length battle dress that had made it so difficult for him to ride during the Suechian raid, Zhao now wore a heavy felt shift under his armor that went to his hips and soft leather trousers. He wore a wrist guard on his left arm and a thumb ring on his right hand. The bow Bulga had crafted hung in a sheepskin case on one side of his mare along with two quivers of fifty arrows, one full of weighted arrows with iron heads, capable of piercing armor; the other of fire arrows, their fire-hardened wooden points wrapped in strips of oil-soaked wool. Fixed to the side of his saddle, behind him so that it did not obscure his vision, a tall, flaming torch roared.

Mogu, too, was dressed for battle. He had exchanged his usual horsehair vest for iron-scale armor, undoubtedly looted from some merchant or unfortunate Han soldier. He wore thumb rings on both hands and wrist guards on both arms so he could shoot with the bow in either hand. Like Zhao, Mogu had two quivers loaded with arrows and a flaming torch fixed to his horse. The Ghuezi had sacrificed a horse to the sky god Tengri the night before, and its dried, rusty brown blood was still crusted on Mogu's flame-lit face.

Mogu and Zhao both had saddlebags brimming over with dried grass, tied into bundles with horsehair twine. They were riding straight for the camp of the Suechian, making much better time than they had on their last expedition now that they knew its location.

"Today is the day we shall find out how much Tengri loves me!" Mogu shouted, his words barely audible over the thunderous noise of the nearly four hundred hooves of all the Ghuezi horses galloping behind them.

Zhao grinned, the flood of excitement that always washed over him before battle was reaching a peak. His mare galloped and he felt perfectly in tune with her. He had never experienced such a connection to an animal before. She was as an extension of his body, responding to his slightest motion with the immediacy of an old lover.

"For Bulga! For Gan Ying! For the Ghuezi!" Zhao cried at the top of his lungs as they galloped into the Suechian camp.

"For the fucked fathers!" Mogu shouted.

The Ghuezi forces charged wide of the Suechian camp, but Mogu and Zhao broke off, riding straight into the middle, galloping between the tents. They both began grabbing bundles of grass from their saddlebags, lighting them with their torches and tossing them into the Suechian camp. Some landed on tents and singed the felts while a few started considerable fires, however, most fell in the grass and produced a lot of smoke but little damage.

Mogu fired his bow into some of the Suechian who were milling around the village, beating felt or milking goats. He knocked one boy clean off his horse with an arrow and whooped. Zhao picked off two muscular, mounted men with a pair of successive shots that pierced them both in the abdomen. Within minutes, though, the cry had gone up and Suechian warriors had mounted. They began shooting arrows back at the two attackers.

Zhao and Mogu urged their mounts away when the Suechian began to organize. They rejoined the Ghuezi, dropping burning grass bundles behind them as they went. Six of the warriors chased after Zhao and Mogu, and Mogu pulled to the side and presented the broadside of his horse to the six warriors.

"Mogu! Stick to the plan!" Zhao shouted, but Mogu ignored him.

The warriors shot at Mogu. He leaned just barely out of the path of one arrow, but Zhao's heart leapt when he saw another hit Mogu in the shoulder.

"Mogu!" Zhao shouted as he saw the arrow connect. Mogu had an integral part to play in the battle plan — if he fell now, everything would be ruined.

But no sooner than Zhao had opened his mouth did he see that the arrow had struck at a lucky angle. It glanced off Mogu's armor instead of piercing it, flying harmlessly up and away. Mogu immediately dipped low in his saddle, swinging and twisting himself around his horse in an unbelievable contortion so that he was riding from the side, his horse's body between himself and the enemy. He proceeded to fire an impossible series of six arrows from under the chin of his own horse, each one burying itself in a Suechian warrior.

"That was incredible, Mogu!" Zhao said, when Mogu pulled back near him.

"It is being nothing, honored guest," Mogu said, grinning broadly.

"I thought I'd mastered horseback archery," Zhao said, shaking his head, "but I see I've still got a lot to learn."

They slowed to a light trot to rest the horses once they had put some distance between themselves and the Suechian camp. It was not long before the dust column put up by the galloping horses of the Suechian horde could be seen behind them, obscured only partially by the several steep hills and short cliffs.

"They're all charging out at once," Zhao said. "I expected we'd have more coming after us individually, like those six you killed. They're more organized than I'd anticipated."

"So? This is being a good thing, surely," Mogu said. "All together they are easier to being killed."

"Perhaps." Zhao paused and stared at the column of dust. It was very wide and very high. "There are more than you told me," he said eventually, "about a thousand."

"The chief of the father-fucking Suechian is probably getting more warriors to fight for him," Mogu said. "Making alliances or conquering other tribes."

"You know their chief?"

"Am I saying that I know their chief? No!" Mogu barked, suddenly defensive. "I am only saying that this is what he must have done."

Zhao did not reply.

"It is what I would be doing," Mogu added, a moment later.

"Are you ready for the next maneuver?" Zhao asked.

"I am being ready," Mogu grinned, "but this is being the dangerous part, yes? If death comes for us today, it will be now."

"If it's the will of Heaven for us to fall, we shall. If it's the will of Heaven for us to succeed, we shall. All things are as they're meant to be, it's for us only to accept them without resistance."

"I mean for the Suechian father-fuckers to die. So I am making that be. Kyah!" Mogu urged his mount forward, directly towards the oncoming horde.

The Suechian forces were hidden in the smokescreen created by the burning grass bundles, only detectable by the high column of dust kicked up by their horses. Zhao and Mogu were leading the charge, a hundred horses behind them but still outnumbered ten to one. When the barest outlines of the forms of the Suechian became visible through the smoke, arrows began buzzing through, missing Zhao and Mogu sometimes by a hair's breadth alone. No Ghuezi arrows were fired back.

"Turn!" Zhao cried.

Mogu's voice and about half a dozen others repeated the order, but the rest of the Ghuezi were silent. The only noises were the whinnies of the horses and the pounding, rhythmic beat of their hooves on the dirt. The Ghuezi herd turned to the right, presenting their flank to the enemy. But the Suechian were too close for a feigned flight maneuver to be pulled off without injury, and the entire left flank of the Ghuezi was peppered with arrows.

A roar went up from the Suechian as they saw, vaguely, through the smokescreen that their arrows had struck so many human shapes. The horses, for the most part, were unharmed and galloped away with their dead riders still atop their backs.

The Suechian pursued, but the Ghuezi were able to put distance between them. The Suechian had been galloping since departing their camp and the Ghuezi had given their horses some time to rest, so they had the advantage. The Ghuezi were not completely out of range, though, and hundreds of Suechian arrows rocketed into their back ranks.

"The father-fuckers are shooting high, trying to kill the men, not the horses, so they have some prize to capture after the battle," Mogu said.

Zhao looked back and saw that Mogu was indeed right, precious few horses had been hit with arrows.

"There! The bundles we planted, shoot them!" Zhao shouted to Mogu.

Bundles of grass had been distributed across the planned route of retreat by the other Ghuezi before the battle could be seen out on their flanks. They were not much larger than those Zhao and Mogu carried and sat far away, at the edge of an arrow's range. Zhao and Mogu, undaunted, reached for their fire arrows, lighting them on their torches and shooting the distant bundles at full gallop. Zhao shot flaming arrow after flaming arrow with unfailing accuracy, putting his hard-won new skill to use.

"Look!" Mogu shouted to Zhao, pointing to the left flank.

Zhao looked, and far out on their left flank he could see riders — riders that must be Suechian. Zhao looked to his right and saw the same thing. Peering through the smokescreen, just barely, Zhao could see that the Suechian formation had stretched out from a thick column into a long, thin, C-shaped line, beginning to encompass the tight Ghuezi formation.

Suechian arrows began to come from the tips of the C, landing perilously close to Zhao and Mogu but missing — missing with incredible accuracy. The arrows were only coming from one direction — the left.

"They're trying to steer us to the right!" Zhao shouted at Mogu.

"Where to?" Mogu asked.

Zhao pointed. To the right, up ahead, was the biggest cliff in the area. Tremendously wide, it had a gentle slope on the far side but a sharp, long drop on the near side. It was so steep that it might have been the wall of a great city. Zhao and Mogu had only two options: ride into the hail of arrows coming from their left or ride towards the dead end of the monstrous cliff.

"Ride towards the cliff!" Zhao shouted. "Then drop your weapons and surrender."

Mogu did not respond and Zhao only hoped he had the good sense to follow his instructions.

As they approached the cliff, they stopped shooting their fire arrows and slowed their horses to a trot, then a walk, riding right up to the cliff, responding to the unspoken orders of the Suechian arrows.

The Suechian C-formation closed in around them, a huge mass of at least a thousand mounted warriors, each one with an arrow in his bow, ready to slaughter the Ghuezi riders like sheep and take their horses as prizes.

Except there were no Ghuezi riders. Zhao allowed himself a smile as he saw revelation dawn on the faces of the enemy warriors, one after another. They began to whisper, and then to shout — some in outrage, but others in confusion. Some of the warriors even laughed.

Only Zhao, Mogu, and half a dozen other Ghuezi were riding horses, guiding the obedient herd. The rest of the horses were mounted by man-shaped hunks of felt, tied together with horsehair twine and peppered with Suechian arrows.

"Now!" Zhao bellowed at the top of his lungs.

That instant, men popped out from around the edges of the cliff and pulled on half-buried stakes. Two long fences of spears shot up from the dirt and were held at an angle, surrounding the cliff in a triangle that captured the felt-men riders of the Ghuezi, but also the surrounding mass of Suechian warriors, in an inescapable pen.

The Suechian fired at the men who had pulled on the ropes at the corners of the cliff, hitting a few before they could duck behind heavy shields. Then a rain of arrows and stones fell on the back ranks of the Suechian. Ghuezi warriors lined the tops of the cliff, with many more missiles ready for the Suechian. A few Suechian tried to fire upwards, and one Ghuezi stone thrower was struck, but most of the arrows they shot came back down upon themselves.

One Suechian rider on the outer ranks urged his horse to turn and tried to jump the spear-fence, but there was not enough space to build up the speed required for such a jump. The poor horse's belly was slashed open by the spearheads and the beast collapsed upon landing, bleeding and screaming. The rider was picked off by a Ghuezi arrow as he tried to flee on foot, as were some other Suechian who attempted to abandon their own horses by leaping from their saddles over the fence.

"Giving up, Khaku! You are being defeated!" Mogu shouted.

"Khaku?" Zhao said, turning to Mogu. "Your brother?"

A voice bellowed from within the ranks of the Suechian. "Putting your bows down and dismount!"

The voice was as deep and authoritative as any war drum Zhao had heard on the battlefield. The speaker was a huge shirtless man with sun-seared skin and not an ounce of fat on him. His shoulders looked like rice pots and his back was as broad as an ox, yet his face had the same squashed quality that Mogu's did — Khaku.

"You told me your brother was dead," Zhao said to Mogu.

Mogu did not give any indication he had even heard Zhao. His eyes were fixed on the hulking form of Khaku, drinking in his every step, studying his face. Mogu was savoring this moment.

Khaku dismounted first and dropped his bow. He walked towards Mogu, who remained on his horse. Slowly, one by one, the Suechian got off their horses and dropped their weapons, too, following the lead of their chief.

"Mogu, this trap is your doing?" Khaku asked him, sounding more impressed than distressed.

"Yes," Mogu answered from atop his horse.

"You are defeating a tribe ten times the size of yours, and you are doing it almost without shooting an arrow."

"Honored guest is saying, 'The supreme art of war is to be defeating the enemy without fighting.'" Mogu responded.

"Actually, Mogu, I was not the one who —" Zhao began, but Khaku's sonorous voice cut him off.

"Well, brother, it is appearing I was being wrong. The Suechian are defeated, you and the other exiles are being worthy of being with us after all."

"Exiles?" Zhao asked, but both Mogu and Khaku were still ignoring him.

"Perhaps I am killing you now and becoming chief of both the Suechian and the Ghuezi," Mogu said.

"This is being your right as the victor," Khaku replied without malice. He was either completely sure that Mogu would do no such thing or completely unperturbed by the prospect of death.

Mogu paused, drinking in his brother's surrender, before eventually speaking.

"I am not killing you, brother, if you are accepting my terms. The Ghuezi and the Suechian are joining together and I am ruling now. You are being my second. Keeping your wives and horses." Zhao noted a little tension left Khaku's shoulders at this, perhaps the elder brother was more worried than he pretended.

"But," Mogu continued, "you are never, ever challenging my rule and you never trying to take back the Suechian for yourself, or else you are being impaled upon a stake and your horses and wives and children are being burned alive in front of you while you die. If you are swearing to all this before the Blue Sky and the warriors gathered here, if you are giving your word of honor, then you are living. All the Suechian shall be living too." Khaku opened his mouth, as if to accept, but then Mogu spoke again, a slight chill in his voice, "Except the warriors who you are sending after us when we are scouting you days ago. They are killing my dogs and my honored guest is desiring vengeance for Bulga, who they are also killing."

Zhao caused his mare to step forward and raised his hand.

"Great Conquering Chief Mogu of the Ghuezi," Zhao intoned with the same solemnity he would use to address a victorious general. "I don't want this. When Bulga died, I felt great anger. I vowed to take vengeance, yes, but I did so without thought and in passion. It's my considered, heartfelt desire not to kill your prisoners. Confucius said, 'Before you embark on a journey of revenge, dig two graves.' Killing them in cold blood wouldn't bring Bulga back, it would only stain my honor and sully your victory."

Mogu accepted this with a nod and motioned Zhao away.

Khaku made the requested vow, and his riders surrendered their weapons to the Ghuezi. Each man and woman among them lined up to repeat an oath of allegiance to Mogu individually, bowing before him and swearing to defend his life with their own, swearing to ride with him wherever he went, and to obey his orders in battle.

Zhao stood by and watched the solemn ceremony respectfully, doing his best to remain patient, but all the time thinking of getting back to the Suechian camp and finding Gan Ying.

CHAPTER SIX

"Who?" Khaku asked, his huge, squashed face flushed red with drunkenness.

Both tribes had gathered together that night around a great fire in the heart of the Suechian camp. They were drinking fermented mare's milk out of horsehair skins and eating the roasted flesh of the horses, rubbed with expensive spices the Suechian had looted from a merchant caravan, that had been killed that day. It was a great banquet to celebrate the ascension of Mogu to the chieftainship of the newly united tribe. Khaku was drinking and feasting as much as any man there, and seemed unbothered by the loss of his position to his younger brother.

"General Gan Ying," Zhao repeated. "He was an envoy from the Protector General Ban Chao. The Suechian attacked his caravan and massacred a company of soldiers. There were several Han scholars traveling with him as well."

"Oh, yes! I am knowing of this man." Khaku took a deep swig of Kumis, shuddered and smacked his lips, then continued. "He is being captured and brought before me."

Zhao could barely contain his elation — Khaku had Gan Ying! Finally, Zhao's arduous quest was at an end. He would be reunited with his master and they could continue on to the lands of the Da Qin, resuming their original purpose after this long distraction.

"Please, where is he?" Zhao asked, climbing to his feet. "Is he unhurt? I must speak to him at once."

"Oh, he is not being here anymore," Khaku said, as if this were obvious. Zhao felt his stomach drop.

"What happened to him?"

"He is showing me the seal of the great Han butcher, so I am letting him be on his way. We are not wanting to provoke Ban Chao." Khaku spoke the name Ban Chao as if he were a wrathful demon. "I am saying to him to be gone and allowing him to keep all his goods and treasures. Even providing him with five of my riders to protecting him around the Desert of Irrevocable Death until he reaches Kashgar. This is happening some time ago, though. He is at least in Kashgar by now, I am thinking. Perhaps beyond."

"Mogu seemed certain that you would detain Gan Ying and the scholars he traveled with," Zhao said. "He said that such men would've been of great use to you."

"Mogu is lying to you, Han man!" Khaku laughed heartily. "Such men are bringing down the wrath of Ban Chao upon us, of what use is this?"

"Mogu suggested they might bargain on your behalf in the oasis trading cities," Zhao said.

"Bah, nonsense! Mogu is just wanting your help with defeating me!" Khaku half-shouted, slapping Zhao heavily on the back with an enormous hand. "And you are giving it to him, yes? He is telling me the strategy he is using to defeat me is yours. Mogu has always known how clever the Han people are. When he is seeing you, I am sure he is saying to himself, 'I am telling this Han man whatever he wants to hear so that he gives me his help.'"

"It seems you're right, Khaku," Zhao said, after a pause, "and it seems this isn't the only thing that Mogu lied to me about."

"Oh?" Khaku raised his thick eyebrows.

"Yes, he told me that you used to lead the Ghuezi, but then you died. He said the Ghuezi were once great warriors, but that the best of them left after your death because they thought Mogu was too young and inexperienced to lead, leaving only the old, the young, and the infirmed. He told me that the Suechian raided them regularly, taking their livestock and women. He didn't say anything about the Ghuezi being exiles or ever having belonged to the Suechian."

Khaku laughed again, spraying Zhao with droplets of fermented mare's milk and spittle.

"These are indeed being lies! Are you not knowing what Ghuezi means in our tongue?"

"No."

"Ghuezi is meaning refuse. Ejecta. That which is abandoned. What is actually happening is Mogu is challenging me for the leadership of the Suechian one day. I am refusing this, of course. Everyone is agreeing he is too young. Everyone is happy with my rule. But Mogu is trying to fight me and I am defeating him easily. Still, he is being my brother. I am loving him. I am not wanting to kill him." Khaku stared off into the fire for a moment, as if revaluating this decision. He then took another long swig of Kumis.

"Benevolence to younger siblings is a sign of virtue," Zhao assured him.

Khaku grunted. "I am saying if he is wanting to be a chief so much, go and do it. Taking those who are not wanted in the Suechian with him. Starting a new tribe of Ghuezi. I am saying this as a joke, but he is doing it! Mogu is taking some goats and horses with him, but some of the Suechian are saying that he is taking too many. So, yes, we are raiding the Ghuezi to get them back. And many of the women who are not liking their husbands

79

are going with the Ghuezi, and their husbands are bringing them back."

"I see," said Zhao. "And when you saw the Ghuezi scouts, you thought they were coming for the women?"

"Yes," Khaku said. "This is why so many men are riding out to chase you off — they are protecting their wives."

Zhao elected not to comment on the questionable use of the word 'protecting.' "Yet Mogu took the people you called refuse and transformed them into a force that defeated your much larger, more experienced, and healthier band of warriors."

"Yes," Khaku said. He stared into the fire again for a long moment. "This is why I am thinking maybe it is not being a bad idea for him to be chief of the Suechian now. Even as a little boy, he is always being ambitious. When he is challenging me and wanting to lead the Suechian, he is only having seen fifteen winters. But perhaps he is having ability to match his ambition. Perhaps he is the one who is to be forming the next great confederation of tribes that will challenge the Han."

"I am sorry I am lying to you, honored guest," Mogu said, bowing his head.

Mogu had ridden out with Zhao, and the two were alone aside from their horses. Mogu looked very different now. No longer did he wear the soft leather leggings and simple horsehair vest that Zhao had grown used to seeing him in. Instead, he wore long, brightly colored but mismatched silks, heavy gold bracelets, and a velvet conical cap. These were riches that had previously belonged to Khaku and, before Khaku, had almost certainly belonged to some poor merchants who made the mistake of taking such valuable trade goods through Khaku's territory.

"I am growing up hearing about the things that the Han generals do. The tricks and strategies they are using to defeat the steppe peoples. And when I am seeing your bravery in battle, I am realizing that you are being the key to winning back my place, and the place of the Ghuezi."

"I forgive you for the deception, Mogu. Confucius said, 'He who refuses to forgive breaks the bridge over which he, too, must one day cross.'"

Zhao dismounted the borrowed mare and held her face close to his. He had grown so attached to her that the realization she would now have to be left behind pained him.

"Thank you, beautiful creature," he whispered to her. "You've been braver and more loyal than most human warriors I've known."

Zhao handed Mogu her reigns but she whinnied and shook her head, stepping backwards away from Mogu. Mogu laughed loudly.

"She is wanting to stay with you!"

The mare stepped to Zhao and nuzzled him with her huge head.

"It appears so," Zhao replied, smiling and petting her head vigorously.

"Then she shall. I am making a gift of her to you, honored guest. I am hoping she is serving you well on your journey to the west."

Zhao enclosed his right fist in his open left palm and bowed deeply to Mogu.

"You honor me, my dear friend."

"What are you naming her?"

Zhao paused for a moment and considered the question. He had never named an animal before.

"Bulga," he said, eventually. "She was a fierce warrior with a gentle soul. This creature shares both those qualities with her."

"A good name," Mogu said, clapping Zhao on the shoulder once he had remounted Bulga.

Mogu stared off into the distance, surveying the large camp of the Suechian, the many nomads scattered out in the vast expanse of grassland surrounding it, grazing their herds and going about their business. His squashed face wrinkled into a deep frown.

"What's worrying you, Mogu?" Zhao asked.

"How am I to be governing all these people, honored guest?" He asked, his voice cracking ever so slightly. "There are being more than a thousand warriors in the tribe, two thousand old people and children. Four thousand horses, four thousand goats, three hundred dogs. This is being a great responsibility. Are you having any more advice for me?"

"The great leaders of the Xiongnu governed an empire of steppe peoples nearly as large as the Middle Kingdom. If that was possible for them, surely you can govern the Suechian," Zhao said.

Mogu nodded, but seemed unmoved.

"They're a belligerent, rough people, Mogu, but they're also sensible and capable. They need what everyone needs from their ruler, protection from enemies and adjudication of disputes. Punish the wrongdoers among them, defeat their enemies, and don't worry about anything else. Lao Tzu said, 'A leader is best when people barely know he exists. When his work is done, his aim fulfilled, they will say they did it themselves.'"

"Hmm, this is being good advice," Mogu nodded thoughtfully, then added, "I am noticing something. It is a small thing, but you are always saying this word, Xiongnu, wrong. You are saying it as *'shong-nue.'* You are saying the last part right but there is no *sh* or *ng* sound. The first syllable is just being said as *'hun.'*"

"Hun," Zhao repeated.

"Yes."

"Well, thank you for correcting my error. So what are your plans for the migration of the tribe? I imagine you'll have to move to new pastures soon."

"I am thinking we are heading west as well. The Han are becoming too strong in the east. Perhaps we are bringing other tribes together on our way. I know that the sister-fucking tribe of the Kuril Nai are being to the west, somewhere. We should be conquering them easily. And many, many more," Mogu's gaze drifted further off to the horizon. Zhao could see in his eyes that the conquest of the Suechian had not been enough for him. In fact, it had just stoked his appetite for more.

"Khaku suggested you might form a new confederacy one day," Zhao said.

"Yes. Yes, one day." Mogu said. "Maybe one day we are raiding these lands of the Da Qin you speak of."

Zhao smiled. "It will take you many years to form a confederacy large enough to challenge that great empire, Mogu."

"Then perhaps it is not being me. Perhaps it is being my sons or grandsons. But perhaps you are staying with us instead of traveling there." Mogu turned away from the rolling grasslands and looked Zhao directly in the eyes. "I was not lying when I was telling you that readers are of great value to the steppe peoples. You are able to be advising me on how to rule. With your wisdom and my fierceness, we are being unbeatable! Together we are defeating a thousand warriors with only one hundred of our own, and barely shedding any blood. Imagine what we are being able to do with the Ghuezi and the Suechian together."

Zhao began to protest, but Mogu held his hand up, asking Zhao to hear him out. "If you are staying with me, we can making the greatest confederacy since Modu Chanyu! You could one day be serving me as the Righteous King of the Right and Khaku will be my Righteous King of the Left." His voice was rising into a crescendo of excitement, and Zhao could almost see the vision building behind his eyes. "We will be searching through the spoils of our raids and furnishing you with the finest mares and geldings, the most beautiful virgins, the best silks and most ornate weapons. When men are riding into battle, they shall be following your every command. When traders are doing business, they shall be following the laws that you decree. Anyone who displeases you is be being impaled before you, and your friends are being raised to wealth and prominence. Your sons will be riding with armies of their own, and your daughters will be marrying great kings and emperors. What are you saying to this?"

For the briefest moment, Zhao allowed himself to entertain the thought. It was not impossible that such a thing could be accomplished. Among the nomadic tribes, birth seemed to matter very little — men followed strength and power. Between Mogu's charisma and Zhao's strategy, with over a thousand horse archers to get them started, it was not inconceivable that the two of them could carve out a kingdom for themselves. A large and powerful one, perhaps.

"I think not, my friend," Zhao said. "As tempting as your offer is, I have a mission of great importance. I must find Gan Ying. I must ensure he gets safely to the lands of the Da Qin."

"But he is already protected by the riders Khaku sent with him, and surely he is finding other warriors who can protect him in Kashgar. He still has treasure and many steppe peoples or warriors of the lands beyond are working for hire. He is not needing you."

"You misunderstand, noble Chief Mogu," Zhao said. "I must be the one to ensure that Gan Ying gets safely to the lands of the Da Qin — me, no other."

"Why?"

"Because once Gan Ying arrives there, I am going to kill him."

AUTHOR'S NOTE

I hope you enjoyed this first installment of the Kung Fu Gladiator series. Li Zhao will be having many more adventures, both in the arena and on the Silk Road. For information on upcoming Kung Fu Gladiator stories, and to check out my other projects, please visit my website: www.bendoublett.com

I have been fascinated with ancient civilizations ever since I was a young boy growing up near the Roman city of Bath in England (should I say Britannia?) but I have to thank Mike Duncan's amazing History of Rome podcast for reigniting my passion for all things Roman. Since marathoning through that series about three years ago, I have buried myself in history books, and I hope that shows in the preceding story. I did have to take certain liberties with historical facts in order to put my story together. Of course, we have no record of any Chinese gladiators. Attentive readers may also note that the Chinese sources record General Ban Chao sent Gan Ying as an emissary to the Parthian Empire, not the Roman Empire. While some speculate that General Gan Ying did reach the Eastern edge of the Roman Empire, formal Sino-Roman relations actually began much later. The earliest Roman emissaries are believed to have reached the Chinese Imperial court during the reign of Marcus Aurelius, some seventy years after the time my story takes place.

Before beginning this project, little else frustrated me more than historical inaccuracies in fiction. There was nothing more painful to my inner critic than watching the Starz show, *Spartacus*. I'm that guy that will sit there, in the movie theater, pointing out every article of clothing that was not available during the period. Don't get me started on *300*. Seriously, ask my friends, I'm obnoxious about it. As a writer, however, I have come to understand that my primary job is to tell a compelling story, not give a factual account of the past. That's the job of professional historians, which I am not. While I have done my best to ensure that I stay as close to the facts as possible, particularly with regard to geography and material culture, astute readers may find other areas where I have had to stretch the historical reality ever so slightly to tell a more compelling story.

I would like to mention a few sources that were particularly helpful to me, and that readers interested in this period might also enjoy as further reading. I made use of several primary sources, particularly excerpts from the *History of the Later Han/Hou Han Shu*, the *Analects of Confucius*, *Sun Tzu's Art of War*, and the *Tao Te Ching*. Further reading included *The Silk Road: Two Thousand Years in the Heart of Asia* by Francis Wood, *Gladiators: 100 BC—200 AD* by Stephen Wisdom, *The Gladiator: The Secret History of Rome's Warrior Slaves* by Alan Baker, *Gladiator: The Roman Fighter's Unofficial Manual* by Phillip Matyszak, *Shadow of the Silk Road* by Colin Thubron, *The Seven Military Classics of Ancient China* by Ralph D. Sawyer, *Handbook to Life in Ancient Rome* by Lesley and Roy Adkins, *Egypt, Greece, and Rome* by Charles Freeman, and *Rubicon* by Tom Holland.

I also relied upon several excellent Great Courses series put together by the Teaching Company: *Great Minds of the Eastern Intellectual Tradition* by Prof. Grant Hardy, *The Other Side of History: Daily Life in the Ancient World* by Prof. Robert Garland, *From Yao to Mao: 5000 Years of Chinese History* by Prof. Kenneth J. Hammond, *Foundations of Eastern Civilization* by Prof. Craig G. Benjamin, *History of the Ancient World: A Global Perspective* by Prof. Greg S. Aldrete, *The Barbarian Empires of the Steppe* by Prof. Kenneth W. Harl, *The History of Ancient Rome* by Prof. Garrett G. Fagan, *Rome and the Barbarians* by Prof. Kenneth W. Harl, *Cities of the Ancient World* by Prof. Steven L. Tuck, *Famous Romans* by J. Rufus Fears, *Greece and Rome: An Integrated History of the Ancient Mediterranean* by Prof. Robert Garland.

A special shout out to the previously mentioned podcast by Mike Duncan as well as the *Life of Caesar* podcast by Ray Harris Jr and Cameron Reilly, who give a hilarious amateur account of the most compelling period of Roman history that is not entirely ruined by the Chomskyite perspective of one of the hosts. Dan Carlin's *Hardcore History* podcast, the *Wrath of the Khans* and *Steppe Stories* series specifically ignited my interest in steppe nomads and inspired the latter half of this story.

    I would like to thank my oldest friend, Joseph Sutton, for his continued support and the inspiration his skill as a story teller has given me over the years. Moriah Pearson, as well, deserves my thanks for the many helpful suggestions she gave the initial draft of this story and her excellent editing services. If you would like to contact her for further information regarding any of the book and editing services she offers, you can email her at moriahpearson@gmail.com. And, finally, I would like to thank my parents for their undying support of my writing and for reading my scribblings ever since I started making them.

Ben Doublett is the owner of a bounce house rental company in Cincinnati, Ohio, where he lives with his three-year-old Great Dane, Freya. He studied Tae Kwon Do for five years and earned a temporary first degree black belt. He became interested in history when he was growing up near the Roman city of Bath in England, and his interest was reignited when he began listening to history podcasts and audiobooks while hiking with his dog. Ben has been writing fiction on and off since early childhood but Kung Fu Gladiator: Volume I is his first published work.

Printed in Great Britain
by Amazon